IN EVERY LIFETIME

IN EVERY LIFETIME

A **TITAN GROUP**
ROMANTIC SUSPENSE

AMY COLE

atmosphere press

To Jeremiaha

My husband, Jeremiaha, has been my guy for most of my life. His sense of "whatever comes our way, we'll handle it together" gave me the courage to try to get the words and stories out of my head and into books. Thank you for your unwavering support, your humor, and our boys.

To my family and friends: thank you. You all are the best part of my life, thank you for being you. Without you, this would never have happened.

Lastly, to the readers, thank you. I've been a voracious reader since I was fourteen and have never wavered in my love of a great romance or a little mystery. I hope I gave that to you in these pages and for just a few hours, you're swept up in Max, Violet, Blitz, and their friends.

PS: To my own Blitz, I love you, sweet girl. Rest easy.

Author's Note

This is the first book of the Titan Group series. Each member of Titan Group will have his own standalone happily ever after, yet reading the books in order will provide the most enjoyment.

All of our heroes in this series have served their country and are retired from active duty. This book, the story of Max and Violet, is the first story to launch the series. Our heroines are all smart, capable women and are equal matches for their heroes. You'll read about love, some spicy scenes, friendship, brotherhood, loyal animals, and a little bit of mystery. Thanks for beginning this journey with me.

CHAPTER ONE

VIOLET

If it wasn't for the breeze swirling through the party and the ability to take a deep breath of fresh autumn air, she would have thought she was back in DC and not overlooking the battlefields of Saratoga in upstate New York. This party had all the markings of the DC scene, senators glad-handing for money, glittering gowns, cigar smoke wafting from smuggled Cuban cigars in the corners, and, of course, the effervescent champagne. The tight, shimmering evening gown scratching across her sensitive arms was completely out of character for her, but, hey, she could dress up if she needed to, complete with a salon-worthy blowout and smokey eye makeup. Truly, she had gone all out, down to the killer heels pinching her feet.

It really was a DC-type feat to essentially re-create a ballroom overlooking a battlefield. She couldn't deny the effect either, it really was a beautiful early fall night, and the battlefield added a layer of romance and mystery that felt like a storybook setting. The flickering torches staked out along the dance floor created on the overlook patio acted as a flame barrier to the darkness beyond, darkness that she knew held the historical paths of the battle sites and encampments of both American and British soldiers. She loved this place and its history. She stiffened her spine in resolve to continue her new adventure of writing her first novel.

After all, she was here for inspiration for the novel she'd

dreamed of writing. If the words didn't start flowing soon, she'd have to go back to work for the *Constitution Now*, the newspaper she'd been working at for the last seven years of her life. She didn't think she could write one more fluff piece on an up-and-coming politician to save her life.

She set her crystal glass on a passing waiter's tray and took out her phone. She might as well take a snap for Hazel or she'd never believe that she'd actually come up here kitted out as she was. She powered up her phone and opened Snapchat, pressing her thumb to the circle icon and slowly, inconspicuously trying to capture the evening. She added a little color commentary about how the canapés could have used some spice and then panned the phone back to her own face.

"I even added a nude lipstick to the smokey eye! Told ya I'd do it." She smiled brightly into the camera and tried to send it off to Hazel. And crap, of course, the internet wasn't working well out here. They probably had some type of jammer with the level of DC power in attendance here. Security had been tight when she climbed the stairs up to the overlook and she wasn't surprised her snap wasn't going through. She quickly saved the snap, turned her phone back off, and slid her phone into her purse. She'd send it later. In fact, she was ready to leave now anyway, might as well find her errant blind date and feign tiredness to get back to her hotel in Saratoga Springs.

She spied him across the dance floor, chatting with another man at their table. Wasn't that Ambassador Neil? She had to hand it to Brandon, her date for the evening, he certainly knew everyone. Of course, he was the Speaker of the House's son, so that was to be expected. That was actually why she accepted the blind date set up by her old editor, an entry into this exclusive party she'd never be able to attend on her own. Brandon was connected, and handsome; his parents were major donors for the fundraiser this evening. He'd been a complete gentleman, even if a little disengaged. There was something about him that made her uncomfortable though, so she was anxious to get back to her hotel, change into those cozy sweats, write notes about the party this evening, and then indulge in yet more *The Office* reruns.

"There she is, my stunning date." Brandon tossed his arm across her shoulders as she joined him and Ambassador Neil. "Sir, this is Violet Burke, a writer for *Constitution Now* and my date for the evening."

Violet extended her hand and offered a polite greeting to Ambassador Neil. He was handsome, late fifties, and the third man in his family to be an ambassador.

"The pleasure is all mine, Violet. What do you think of the fundraiser this evening? Did you know that we are almost at the 247th anniversary of the Battle of Saratoga Springs?" He still held her hand from their introduction.

"It's beautiful, sir, truly. I did know that. The battle started September 19, right?" She gently pulled back on her hand and replied lightly, not sure if she should demur or be honest in her knowledge.

"Ah, you've found yourself a keeper, Brandon, well done." Ambassador Neil winked at Brandon. "Yes, and it lasted until October 7. It was a decisive victory for the American troops. In fact, it should come as no surprise to you that my own great-great-great-grandfather was here during the battle." He gave that polished smile again.

"How wonderful. You must be so proud." She demurred, turning back to her date.

"I was actually hoping you were perhaps ready to go, Brandon." *Please say yes*, she pleaded with her eyes, soft smile firmly affixed to her face. She chuckled and self-deprecatingly added, "I even took a little video for my sister." She turned back to Ambassador Neil. "To capture how magical the evening has been, sir."

She felt Brandon's soft hand tighten on her shoulder. That was odd. Was that a flash of irritation across his handsome features? Brandon smiled down at her. "Sure, Violet, let's head out." He nodded to Ambassador Neil. "Neil, a pleasure, as always."

"Well, Violet, it was nice to meet you. You'll have to come by our event back in the city next week." Ambassador Neil kissed her hand, clapped Brandon on the shoulder, and waved hello to another guest as he moved to join them.

Brandon really was a decent blind date; she just didn't feel any connection. Perhaps that was fine though, that hadn't been her goal for tonight anyway. He was too polished, too much the typical DC trust fund baby for her to feel comfortable with. She didn't have the sense that she was his type either. Small-town aspiring novelist currently living in DC, cosmopolitan she was not.

They made small talk on the way to the car, through the buckling in and on the drive back into town. He seemed almost pensive, and she briefly wondered what he and the ambassador had been talking about. She was relieved to see the lights of town coming into focus. They were passing the dark mass of the springs park when headlights streaked across the rearview mirror. The car behind them felt super close all of a sudden, and she reached her left hand toward the console to steady herself, right as their car was hit from behind hard.

"Brandon!" she yelled. What was happening? There had been rampant drinking at the party, but they were some miles away from that now and almost back in Saratoga Springs.

"Shit! Hold on, Violet, that fucker!" Brandon seemed both incensed and shocked. His hands were gripping the wheel tighter as the car behind them eased back and swerved into the road. She felt her breathing coming in pants, they were really close to the curve leading onto the main street, and the darkness was coming up on them fast. She grabbed the door handle as hard as she could, her muscles tense, her eyes flashing at the rearview mirror as the car behind them sped up again and hit them a second time. Their car was spinning!

She heard the crunch before she felt anything. Was she alive? Her body felt numb and there was screaming in her ears, then nothing. She risked a glance at Brandon, he was unconscious, head on the wheel, blood trickling down an ugly gash in his head. His breathing was low, but he was alive. She felt his wrist for a pulse and tried to slow her own racing heart. They needed help. She didn't know what had happened. Had the driver behind them been drinking? Where did he go? Her throat felt hoarse, so she assumed the screams had been her own.

Her little clutch, which she thought was so fun just a couple of hours ago, still dangled from her wrist from its little strap. She tried to open it, she knew her phone was in there, and she needed to call for help. It took several tries, she couldn't get her fingers to work, damn it! She finally got it out and powered it on.

"Nine-one-one, what's your emergency?" The dispatch trilled through the silent car. Oh, thank God, finally, she was able to connect.

"Yes, we've been in an accident, um, we're by the entrance to the springs park. We've been hit. My friend, my friend needs help, please!" Violet gave as many details as she could to the woman on the other end of the line. She stayed on until she heard the sirens in the distance. Relieved and doing her best to keep a running commentary to try to wake Brandon, she didn't stop rambling until the paramedics pulled the car door back to get her out. She turned off her phone again, knowing she'd need the battery to call Hazel as soon as she possibly could, and not knowing when she'd be back at her hotel to charge it.

She could see that Brandon's side of the car had taken the brunt of the accident. Her arm was burning, but she did an internal check of everything else and knew she was OK.

She tried to walk back through what happened while the EMT checked her out and people started to gather. Brandon was loaded onto a stretcher, awake now but dazed.

"Miss, you're clear. It looks like just the cuts on your arm, but otherwise, you were really lucky. This could have been so much worse." The paramedic finished cleaning out the bits of glass from her arm and cleaned the wounds up. "Your friend wasn't as fortunate as you were, we need to get him to the hospital for more tests, but he is asking for you."

"OK, thank you. Thank you, thank you so much." Violet felt like she was watching herself thank the man and walked over to the stretcher Brandon was laid out on. She squeezed his hand as he opened his eyes.

"Violet, go, I'm fine. I'll be OK. Really. Go back to your hotel and I'll call you tomorrow. I'm going to be fine, I'm sure it's protocol because I napped a bit back there. Really, go back to the hotel and get some rest."

"Only if you're sure, Brandon, I don't want to leave you alone." She really did hate to leave him, even if he was a blind date she'd spent a total of forty-five minutes alone with. But geez, she would love to get to those sweats and some sleep. Her adrenaline was crashing, and she felt so drained.

"Yes," he squeezed her hand again, "I'll call ya. Really." He dropped her hand as the EMTs began to load him into the back of the ambulance. She watched until they closed the big doors and turned to the policeman off to her side.

"Ma'am, if you're ready, I'd like to take a statement tonight but I promise to get you home quickly. We can follow up tomorrow as long as I get the basics tonight. I'll even drive you back to your home or hotel." He looked young but earnest and friendly, and really, she felt relieved for the offer.

"Yes, OK, that sounds good. Although, I don't really know that I can tell you much. I think the driver must have been drinking. They hit us twice, but I think I saw them swerving too. It was a small SUV, dark. Are they here?" She turned her head and scanned the scene of onlookers and emergency responder vehicles for a smaller, dark SUV while the cop walked her to his cruiser. He held the front passenger door open for her and replied.

"No ma'am, there were no other vehicles when the first responders arrived. You said a dark, small SUV?" He paused to write that down in his notepad once he got her settled in the seat.

"I think so, but I don't see it now either. It must have some damage also. I really hope that they don't hit someone else tonight. I can't believe they didn't stop, but I suppose if they were drinking, they were scared to stop." Insane behavior in her book, but drinking and driving was also not something she considered, so what did she know? He asked her a few more questions and took down her information before he put the car in drive.

He drove her back to The Adelphi, the Grecian hotel on the main street of the old, fabled town. He pulled up in front of the hotel, slid the cruiser into park, and hopped out to get her door. He held it open for her as she got out and handed her his card.

"Well, that's not the welcome we try to give visitors, and please, call me or text me if you think of anything else before we talk tomorrow. Get some rest and I'll be back around 8:30 in the morning. We can grab coffee in the lobby, my treat, and we'll finish up your statement."

"Thanks, officer. I'll see you in the morning." She gratefully shook his hand before turning back into the lobby of her hotel. The lights were low, and she felt like it had been hundreds of years since she'd dressed up and met Brandon in the lobby. She gambled that her battery would last until she could plug in now that she was so close to her room, and pulled out her phone, holding the button until it flared to life. A quick glance at the time revealed it was barely after 11:00, not even five full hours had passed! She quickly brought the phone to her face to open it, hit Hazel's number, and listened to the ringing as she walked through the dim lobby toward her room.

"Vi! How was your fancy-pants party and your dashing date?" Hazel's bright voice enveloped her.

"Oh Hazey, I'm OK, so don't freak, but we were in a car wreck!" Violet started to tell Hazel all about it as she approached her room. As she got nearer, she noticed that the door was slightly open. And was that noise inside of her room? She knew she didn't leave the door open, she always checked that. Her head was pounding now, too much excitement for one evening.

She lowered her voice, "Shit, Hazey, I think I'm in trouble. I gotta go."

CHAPTER TWO

VIOLET

"Vi!" She could hear Hazel protesting as she hit "end" and slid the phone back into the wristlet still dangling from her uninjured arm. She wasn't an idiot; she knew she shouldn't go in there by herself. She was running through scenarios to try when she heard two deep, murmuring voices.

"She'll be back any minute and we'll do it then, relax." OK, this wasn't good. They had to be talking about her, and while she didn't know what was happening, she knew it was off. She started to back away from the door. If only she was wearing her Brooks and not these dang heels! She was almost back around the corner when her phone started buzzing like crazy in her purse, which was inconveniently flush to the wall she was attempting to slither down. She heard the voices again as she darted around the corner and did the first thing she thought of, hid on the bottom of a serving cart left at the mouth of the hallway. She had just settled the thick, cream-colored tablecloth on the cart around herself when she felt the thudding of heavy boots.

"It had to be her, the cop just left her off. Shit. We can't lose her or we're dead too."

"She can't have gone too far, man, don't call bossman yet. You check the park across the street and I'll go around the building."

She was convinced that any second they would hear her heart trying to beat out of her chest. And also, she would now not be running into the park for shelter, thank you very much. Damn, that had been her plan.

She waited for them to disperse and then she gently pulled her phone out. Should she call Officer Waite? The guy with the boots had known when the officer had dropped her off, could she trust him? And also, what in the hell was going on here?!

Her screen lit up and she glanced back down.

Hazel: Vi
Hazel: VIOLET!
Hazel: VIOLET KAY BURKE. You better answer me right now or I am calling the cavalry.

Luke: Vi? You good?
Luke: Vi, Hazey is blowing up my phone, where are you?

Hazel: You gave me no choice.

That earned an eye roll. Her phone vibrated in her hand again, Luke calling. She pressed the green button and hissed out a hello.

"Luke, I think I stepped in it but I don't know what. Um, but really, can't talk now, I'm hiding from two guys I get the sense are very bad and I've been in an accident, but I'm OK. I'm starting to freak out a bit, not gonna lie."

"Vi, I'm sending help, and then you can tell us all what the fuck is going on. Where are you?"

"Um, sure thing, Luke. Really hope to be alive to tell you, but, um, not getting a good feeling about that."

"Violet, listen to me. I've got the schematics of the building pulled up now. Go to the cleaning supply closet on the top floor. Barricade the door once you're there. I'm sending help. I have a teammate in Lake George and he'll be there within the hour. Listen to me, barricade the door and don't open it until you hear the word 'Nutella.'"

"Luke, I'm scared. Also, Nutella?"

"Ya, Vi, Nutella. Listen to me, do not go back into your room, go straight to that cleaning supply closet, barricade yourself in, and wait for Max. It's going to be OK, but you have to listen here. Get there now. You only have a short window before anyone after you circles back. Hang up, turn off your phone, get to that closet on the top floor, and wait for Max."

"Love you, Luke, got it. Nutella."

"Nutella, Vi, love you."

She powered her phone down and slid it back into her wristlet, tried to quiet her breathing, counted to twenty to see if she heard anything, and then very gently lifted the tablecloth covering the serving cart. It looked clear. Cripes, it was now or never apparently. She sent up a little prayer that she made it upstairs OK and that Luke's intel was good. He was a Marine special forces leader, so she had to trust him.

Once in the supply closet on the top floor, she barricaded the door with the sturdiest mop she could find and hid behind some linens. It wasn't great, but it would have to do. She sure hoped whoever Max was, he got there fast.

CHAPTER THREE

MAX

Blitz was right next to him, step for step. The poor dog had started to look at him with pleading eyes to stop about three miles back, but, hell, he hadn't begun to quiet the voices yelling in his head. The dog would do anything to veer off course and take a moonlit swim in Lake George any moment of any day though.

"Sorry, bud, not yet."

His phone vibrated in his chest pocket. What the hell? It was late, and a late phone call never meant anything good.

He pulled the phone out and stabbed the green button, "Luke, what part of 'leave me alone' was tricky for you?" He couldn't take any more of his well-meaning friend right now, but Luke had been his team lead, and when your commanding officer called, you answered, active duty or not.

Luke was more brother in arms, forged in blood, but, hell, he couldn't hear more platitudes right now from Luke about how it wasn't his fault his own literal brother, Alex, was dead, along with three others from their Raiders special forces team.

"Max, I need you." Luke was in operator mode, Max heard it in his voice. He slowed and felt Blitz do the same at his calf.

"Go," he clicked into the same mode with Luke. He'd never not answer a call for help from Luke.

"Listen, Hazel's sister Violet is in trouble. I don't know what the hell is happening, but she's been run off the road and she is hiding now from guys after her. She's holed up at The

Adelphi in the Springs, top floor, cleaning closet. She's barricaded in, but I don't know how long that will keep her hidden or safe. Unknown scope here, unknown tangos."

Max was in motion as he listened to Luke, cutting through town back to his little motel room on the water. It was the fastest way to his truck, but he was still twenty-seven miles from the Springs.

"You need to get to her, code word Nutella." Luke finished. "Max?"

"Got it, Luke, I'm on it. I'll get her and get somewhere safe. I'll check in when we're solid."

"Thanks, buddy. Listen, Violet, she's like a sister to me man. I don't know what is going on but I need her safe."

"Luke, buddy, I got you. But Nutella, what the fuck is that man?"

Luke chuckled through the line. "Just get there. And thanks, man, call me when you're good." He clicked off.

"Let's go, Blitz, Luke needs us."

He made it to The Adelphi in twenty-three minutes. Thankfully, he'd never eased up on his training and the run back to his truck hadn't taken long. Blitz was alert in the seat next to him, watching. The dog knew operator mode just as well as they all did.

He'd grabbed a go bag from his room, not sure what to expect. He pulled into the twenty-four-hour diner a block down from The Adelphi and parked his truck. He holstered his gun against his chest and slid on a hooded zip-up, scanning the area.

Leashing Blitz, he clocked his surroundings. A young couple at the counter in the diner, a group of college students studying in the corner booth, and a waitress at the register laughing with a group of women paying their tab. He started whistling and stopped to apologize to Blitz under his breath. Obviously, Blitz didn't need a leash, but it fit the ruse of the moment. Max's specialty was blending in. With a zippered sweatshirt, his six-foot, four-inch frame seemed smaller. His Georgia Tech hat, tennis shoes, and running pants gave the appearance of a guy out for a late night run with his dog, which he had literally been less than thirty minutes ago. No one seeing him now would look askance at this outfit. The late hour was good for him too, his dark hair and the scruff on his face less intimidating if everything was dark.

He broke into a jog, pretending to check an earbud while he hit his stride, Blitz alert and focused alongside him. As he approached her hotel, he made a little show, talking to Blitz about needing to stop to use the restroom.

"Sorry, buddy, I shouldn't have had that last protein shake. Gotta stop in here and hit the restroom." Max rolled his eyes at himself. Who would talk to their dog about that in real life? He spotted four guys in the block of the hotel, all possible tangos. It was clear they were talking to each other on comms.

As he got closer to the door, he made sure to wave to the guy milling about the front area. "Hey, man, I gotta lay off the protein shakes before runs, right? Think they'll care if I use the head in the lobby?" Max made his voice even-keeled, lighter, less threatening.

The guy grunted at him and immediately turned around, scanning the entrance to the park again. Max almost chuckled darkly to himself. He almost wanted the guy to engage so that he could take one of these assholes out, but he was on extraction right now and would not engage unless he had to.

Max patted Blitz on the side. "Let's hit the head, boy, and then find you some water to drink." He acted as nonchalant as possible until he rounded the lobby corner, where he quietly closed the door behind him and took the stairs two at a time.

He was at the top floor in no time, knocking on the cleaning supply closet as gently as possible. "Nutella," he murmured. He heard movement against the door and then it opened just a crack. He saw dark waves first, one large hazel eye fixed on him, and one delicate cheekbone. "Nutella," he said again.

"Max?" She opened the door further and he felt the breath catch in his throat. Violet was a beautiful woman. She had on a dark dress that seemed to shimmer as she opened the door further, a riot of dark hair falling against her pale shoulders and, in her hand, was a screwdriver.

CHAPTER FOUR

MAX

"Violet, yes, I'm Max," he said as he stepped inside with her and closed the door behind him. "Luke sent me. I'm going to get you out of here, but we need a plan. I counted four guys on the street and they're on comms with someone. Is the room next to yours occupied?"

She shivered but didn't lower the screwdriver. He put his hand on top of hers to lower it gently. "Vi, right? It's going to be OK. Luke sent me."

That seemed to wake her from the trance she was in. Probably shock. He remembered that Luke had mentioned she'd also been run off the road and he noticed the smattering of cuts across her right forearm. He'd be asking her more about that later. First, they needed to get to a more secure location. Then, then he'd figure out who he needed to kill.

Shaking that possessive thought off, where the hell did that come from? He had just met her. But fuck, Luke had talked about Violet and Hazel for years. He knew these women were like the sisters his buddy had never had and he would always have Luke's back. He asked her again, "Is the room next to yours occupied?"

"No, I don't think so. I just got in last night, but I haven't seen any movement from the room on the right, room 114. I know the room to my left is occupied," She whispered.

"OK, we're going to step into the hallway where my dog Blitz is keeping watch. Once there, I'll lead the way, right in front of you on the stairs and then I'll clear the way to that room. I want you right at my back, don't let go unless someone has you. I need to feel you there to keep moving. We're going to be quick, slipping into that room. Be ready and be alert. Here." He handed her a knife. "Keep this on you. If we get separated, Blitz will be with you and will raise an alarm, but you gut anyone who tries to take you. Push in hard and fast, turn and pull up as hard as you can."

She shivered again. "Blitz?"

"Yes, you'll love him and he won't leave your side. Prepare to get drool on your dress."

She laughed. She loved dogs and she hated this gown at this point. Not to mention these heels. Also, wow, did Luke send her a *GQ* model? Holy hotness. His dark hair curled under his hat and the scruff on his strong jaw looked a couple of days old. His eyes were intense on her, the golden color almost glowing in the low light from under the crack in the door.

"Um, Max, why not my room? I'd love to change out of this dress."

He had a vision of her, sans dress, wild waves around her shoulders, and eyes full of lust instead of fear. What. The. Fuck. He'd known this woman for all of two seconds and was trying to get them out of a trap alive to tell the tale, what the hell was going on with him? It had clearly been too long for him, not that he was like so many of his buddies with women everywhere they went.

"Vi, they've probably been back in your room by now and might return multiple times before they give up, especially if your things are still inside. But they've likely cleared your floor already and won't look right next to where you were again. We can get in, get a plan. I'll try to get you out of the gown as quickly as possible."

Shit. Not like that. Oops. Alex was laughing at him from the grave. Smooth Max, real smooth, he thought to himself.

"Shit, Vi, sorry, I mean that I'll try to get you some different clothes as soon as possible."

She gave a little smirk, but at least the fear was fading from her eyes. She looked like a crazed warrior princess with a screwdriver in one hand and the knife he'd given her in the other. "OK, I can do it. Lead the way." She set the screwdriver back on the shelf behind her and then put her free hand against his back as he turned to open the door to the closet.

Blitz perked up when he saw Max, still alert. Good, Max thought, still clear. Three steps ahead and with his head on a swivel, he led them to room 114. He slid a credit card in and pulled out his own knife to give it a little nudge. They were inside, all three practically pasted to the door within a minute. He checked the peephole, still clear. The hallway wouldn't stay clear for long if these guys were professionals, they would at least do rounds down each hall, and he wasn't taking chances.

He patted Blitz on his side and leaned down to nuzzle his head. "Good boy. Keep us safe." The dog gave a little nuzzle in return and leaned against the side of the door. Ears up and eyes clear.

CHAPTER FIVE

VIOLET

She felt as if she was dreaming. The night had started kind of fun with a gorgeous dress, a fabulous blowout and makeup, a handsome blind date to a glamorous fundraiser in a historical park. What's not to love? Oh yeah, being in a car wreck, being chased, folding herself onto a serving cart to hide from guys with guns and then wedging herself into linens, and brandishing a paltry screwdriver for a defense weapon. All this fun, in one night no less! And now, Tall, Dark, and Dreamy was rescuing her. With his black Lab! What was happening? She'd felt ropes of muscles on Max's back when she pressed against him leaving the closet. The guy seriously worked out.

"Marine, right?" He'd said Luke sent him and Luke said he was a teammate. Oorah indeed. Thank you, Luke, she thought to herself.

"Ya, Luke's team," Max replied quietly. "I'm on a leave, probably permanently, staying up at Lake George. We need to get back to there as quickly as possible but we have to get past the goon squad first. Then, I'm going to need you to tell me why they're after you."

"As soon as I figure that out, you'll be the first to know, I promise." She shivered again, the night was finally hitting her. She was in over her head here. She had read books like this before and it all seemed romantic, but that was brilliant writing from her favorite authors. She knew that now, living it kind of robbed the action of its romance. Although her partners in this were pretty sexy and pretty dang adorable, respectively.

She couldn't stop shaking. "I really have no idea what is happening right now. Seriously. I'm just glad that you are on leave, I guess. Lucky for me, people are trying to kill me so close to Lake George."

Max stepped closer, still quiet and watchful.

"I mean, at least I had the decency to step in something so close to your vacation location. How wonderful for me!" Her whispers were getting higher and higher pitched. "Hey, maybe you could put a tux on and we could dance our way out of here guns blazing."

Strong arms enveloped her. He didn't tighten his arms, but he was solid. She felt his heartbeat against her chest as the zipper on his jacket grated against the skin above the sweetheart neckline of her dress. Tears had gathered in the corners of her eyes, but she sniffed them back.

She felt strong arms sweeping across her back. He was calm and steady. She felt his scruff against her jaw like a warm whisper on her skin. "Shhhhh," he breathed into her ear. "I've got you. We've got you. No one is killing you. I've got you." The hands swept again, warm and reassuring. She focused on the warmth his big hands were infusing into the skin on her back. She shivered again and took a deep breath in through her nose and out through her mouth. One more. Her heart rate started to slow back down and Max stepped back. "Good?"

"Yeah, I think I'm good. For now." She didn't have time to process all that had happened so far.

"Good. I have good news. Your room has a connecting door to this one. I'm going to get you some clothes. I want you to stay here with Blitz and the knife I gave you. I'm going to be in and out. Tell me exactly what you want and where to grab it. We need to be very fast in this, so be as specific as possible. We're going to leave as much as possible so that they don't know anyone has been back in there."

Her Brooks! And a hairband, thank God. She detailed for him where to grab jeans and a sweatshirt, her tennis shoes, and her bathroom bag. Her makeup would be scattered across the counter, but her little bathroom bag still had a disposable toothbrush in it, hair bands, and some Tylenol, perfect for her headache at this point.

Max checked the hallway again, patted Blitz, and checked the connecting door. It sounded quiet throughout the hotel, so he broke in. At a later date, she was going to explore how easy it had been for him to gain access to these rooms in this hotel.

CHAPTER SIX

MAX

He knew Blitz would bark at the first sound of visitors, but he also knew they were on borrowed time. He spied her open bag and the tennis shoes next to it. He rifled through the clothes to get to her jeans and a well-worn sweatshirt.

Still quiet, good. He took in the room around him. A laptop bag and charger were on the desk but no laptop. The room had clothes tossed about, someone had definitely come back in here. Someone was looking for something.

He better wrap this up. He grabbed the bag she'd told him to get from the bathroom counter and was just passing back through the adjoining door when he heard the lock being disengaged on her room.

He pulled the door closed on their side, set her items down behind him, and pulled his gun out, pointed toward the now closed door to her room. He didn't want to engage, but they'd have to kill him and Blitz to get her out of there.

"Where is that bitch?! He is going to kill us if we don't take care of her." The voice was pissed and filled with fear. He heard some muffling.

"Cool it. I'll handle her. She can't have gone far. She's in an evening gown in the middle of nowhere for fuck's sake. Alone. We'll find her." A more authoritative voice. "Go take care of the guy, make sure he doesn't say a word. Permanently. I'll handle the girl."

The guy? What was that about? He really needed to get

them to a secure location and get some details. And now, he potentially had a secondary rescue to figure out. For being on leave, this was getting intense. He hoped there wasn't a husband somewhere he was also going to need to save. He had just met Violet, but the thought that she was married or with someone made his gut clench. Shaking himself, he listened for the guys on the other side to say more or scatter.

Once he knew they were gone, he turned to Violet. Her face was ashen and the fear was back in her eyes. "They're going to kill Brandon?!" She whisper yelled.

"Oh my God. Oh my God. Now I've gotten Brandon killed for whatever I've stepped in?! Max! We have to help him. He's hurt, there's no way he can protect himself."

"Tell me who he is and where he is, I'll see what we can do. Then, we are getting the fuck out of here."

She told him about the blind date, the fancy fundraiser, and the wreck. He watched her closely the entire time, peppering in questions. The relief that swept through him when he realized they weren't talking about a boyfriend or husband was unnerving. Christ, he was such a dick. This guy might die and all he could think about was how Violet didn't seem interested *like that*. Alex probably was laughing his ass off now from wherever he was watching Max fumble this. He shook his head clear and refocused on what she was saying.

"OK, get changed. We've got to get clear of Saratoga Springs. I'm going to call Luke and see what he can do. Listen, Vi, we can't go over to the hospital. I'm not taking you right to the head of the snake."

She opened her mouth like she might argue, thought better of it, pursed her lips, and ran into the bathroom to change. Max called Luke and whispered what he'd learned as quickly as possible. He hung up with assurances that Luke would do what he could to save this Brandon guy and that they would reconnect as soon as they could.

He looked up to see Violet in her sweatshirt and jeans

with her hair pulled back. His breath caught in his throat. What was it about this woman? She'd gone from a shimmering dress that hugged her gorgeous curves with her hair a wild wave around her creamy shoulders to jeans. And a sweatshirt. Fuck, she was getting more and more beautiful. The hit to his head during that last mission must be acting up, he was out of his mind and he barely knew this girl.

"Max? I think I'm ready. Should I leave the dress?"

"Yes, but hide it. We don't want these assholes to know you've got help any earlier than they need to know that. The chance that they search this room too is small but not nonexistent. That's if we can get away without being seen."

She rolled it up and popped it in the microwave, and then turned to him with a shrug. "I'm ready."

CHAPTER SEVEN

VIOLET

She couldn't believe this was her life. Also, she had forgotten to ask Max to get her a regular bra when she sent him for her clothes. Good grief, that felt awkward, so it was probably for the best. He was off the charts hot, not to mention her skin seemed to spark every time she touched his hand or back. Oh, and no small thing, she was being hunted and Brandon was in danger of being killed because of whatever mess she had gotten herself into.

Yet still, the lacy, strapless, black bra that looked great with her black, strapless gown was kind of itchy under her old Georgetown sweatshirt. Who knew she would be running for her life in the gorgeous La Perla creation and its matching black thong? At least she had her Brooks and was able to take off the killer heels. She shook her head at herself. She really was a practical person, but leave it to her to be in her nicest lingerie while being hunted by madmen for God knows what.

She turned to Max. "How are we getting out of here?"

"A blitz." He smirked at her.

At that, she turned to Blitz as the dog left his post by the door and went to Max's side. He leaned into Max's leg and looked up adoringly to get his next command. Max gave Blitz a pat and then met Violet's eyes.

"Thankfully, you're on the main floor, so we're going to use that to our advantage. Blitz is going to go out this window first, quietly. He's going to get friendly with the guard they have in the back and then I'm going to sneak up on him. Once I've incapacitated him, I'll motion for you to get out as fast as you can and get to that tree line." He pointed to the row of pine trees on the side of the parking lot. "From there, we need to work our way back west, toward a twenty-four-hour diner. My truck is in the parking lot, and once we can get to it, we have a little more cover. Like before, I'll stay right ahead of you with Blitz ahead of me. Hang on to me and be ready for anything. You ready?"

She nodded her head. It sounded like a good plan to her, and Max (and Blitz) had gotten them this far. "OK, I'm with you."

"Good, let's go."

The window opened without too much noise, which was the first hurdle. Violet couldn't see much practically pressed against Max's back, but she felt his muscles bunched under her hand. He was focused ahead as was Blitz.

Once the window was slid open enough for them to pass through, she felt Max's hand run along Blitz's back. The dog tensed beside them and then sprang over the window in a silent leap. He cleared the window without a sound. Moments later, she felt Max reach back and squeeze her hand. "Now."

Max seemed to bounce over the window as effortlessly as his dog did and as silently. She watched while he crept through the bushes around the window and across the sidewalk to the parking lot where the man had bent over to shoo Blitz away. Blitz wasn't growling or biting but was acting playful for the man. The man was attempting to push Blitz away and didn't see Max on him until it was too late. Max had his arm locked around the man's neck in a moment, muscles bulging while the man silently fought to stay awake. The man slumped against Max and Max dragged him back into the bushes and then motioned for her to join him. She didn't bound over as her partners had, but she was over and out of the hotel, hand in Max's and hidden in the tree line around the parking lot before the next guard came around the corner. As he worked his way toward where his partner was hidden unconscious in the bushes against the hotel, they worked their way through the pines, heading west toward the diner.

Violet was about to take a breath when she felt Max tense under her hand and come to a sudden stop, watching Blitz at attention a few feet ahead of them.

The dog had stopped, tail pointed straight out, paw lifted slightly. She waited, her own muscles tensed, her fear starting to clog her throat. Thankfully, the dog started to move again, and Max followed his lead. From her periphery, she saw another guard had made his way past them and was catching up with the second guard. Their voices were too low to hear, but they were both also on comms, making it clear that they were aware one of their own was unaccounted for. Blitz had done well to save them; she'd have to remember to get the dog some treats if she made it out of this alive.

They reached the edge of the pine trees. All that remained now between them and Max's truck in the diner parking lot was a side street. There was no cover. She felt Max reach back again and squeeze her hand.

With a voice so low she felt it more than heard it, he said, "The truck is unlocked now. Blitz will be by the driver side, go to that door with me, and be ready to jump in. The chances of us making it there undetected are pretty low, so you need to be ready. Do you remember what I said about the knife?"

"Stab, turn, and pull up as hard as I can." She gulped. How could she forget?

He nodded and squeezed her hand again.

She watched Blitz cross the street, going straight to the truck. She didn't hear any yelling and again she felt Max's muscles bunch right before they took off together at a run that felt more like he was carrying her versus her running behind him.

She heard shouts. They were so close to the truck, but the

shouts were getting louder. Blitz started barking and she heard shots starting to pepper the pavement around her. "Max!" He threw open the door and shoved her inside, Blitz jumping in after her and lying on her as she shrank against the seat. Max had returned fire toward the tree line, but wasn't clear to get in yet.

"Start the truck, Vi! If I say, 'Go,' you need to get out of here. Go toward Lake George and lose yourself in the hills around the lake. Luke will track you if you just stay in this truck. He knows if I don't check in that we hit trouble."

"I'm not leaving you behind, Max. I can't!" Blitz was barking and the shots were ringing in her ears, but she was not leaving Max behind to deal with whatever trouble she had found. She fired up the truck and screamed to Max, "Hang on! Do not let go of that door!"

She didn't know if Max heard her or not but she didn't have time to confirm. He was firing back from behind the door. The window had already been shot out, and he stuck his arm through that to grab on as she hit the gas and the truck shot forward. She didn't know if this would work, but it was their only chance of getting away from these assholes. Blitz was lying low on the bench seat, barking at Max.

Max kept firing as she lurched the truck through the parking lot, trying to swing him inside. As they hit the curb hard, her breath was knocked from her lungs, but it swung Max back around and he was able to jump in with her. She couldn't see anything through Max's big body, but she refused to take her foot off the gas. They careened through the intersection with Max righting himself and her trying to scoot over while keeping the gas strong.

He took command of the truck and pushed her down onto the passenger floorboards. "Get down! Keep your head low!" His hand was on her head one minute and then she felt Blitz lying on her the next. The dog felt like a warm jacket, vibrating against her as she watched Max drive. He had his gun ready and was focused on the road.

"We've got company, Vi, stay down until I can get us out of this."

She nodded, her throat too thick with fear to speak. The truck spun around a corner so hard that her back pressed against the glove compartment. She felt Blitz whine against her throat.

"Me too, boy, me too." She hugged the dog to her, praying they got out of this alive to get him those treats. The truck skidded left and then Max was throwing it in reverse. He hit the lights and slunk down in the seat just enough to see. Moments later, she heard a murmured, "Dumb fuckers."

They were in drive again. This time she felt the truck make a looped turn, heading almost back to the diner all the way before creeping along a tree-lined residential street.

"The truck is too noticeable now, Vi, we need to switch out. Give me a couple of minutes. I want you to stay down until I say it's time, OK? Are you OK?" he asked.

"Yes," she breathed out.

"OK, sweetheart, give me a minute, I've got you." He squeezed her shoulder and patted Blitz's side.

It couldn't have been more than a full minute later and she felt the truck ease into a driveway, shadows reaching across the cab. He put it in park, reached behind him, and grabbed a bag.

"Sweetheart? We need to get out. We're hidden where we are on a fairly dark driveway, but we need to get out quickly and then find a ride close by before these homeowners wonder what an extra truck is doing tucked back by their house."

She nodded and he helped her up. "Are you OK?" she asked him.

"I could ask you the same thing. But yeah, I'm good. You?" he replied.

"Yes, thanks to you and Blitz." She smiled at him, running her fingers through Blitz's soft fur.

"Glad to hear it, Violet, let's roll," he said decisively.

Max, Violet, and Blitz jumped out of the truck, Max closing the door behind them as quietly as he could. He tossed the bag he'd grabbed over one shoulder and held his hand out to her.

She'd known this man for less than two hours now, and they'd been shot at, evaded capture twice, and he'd talked her down from a meltdown, sweeping those big hands across her back and whispering into her ear. He'd come for her without knowing her because Hazel had called Luke and Luke had sent him. All of it without anyone knowing what she had gotten herself into.

She glanced back up and met his eyes. His smile had softened across his face and his eyes sparkled. "M'lady, your chariot awaits." He reassured her with that low voice. She took his hand, something that felt so natural and yet so new. He tucked her against his back and side, offering his body as protection with Blitz leading their way. A pattern that had gotten a little too familiar in such a short time.

Three houses over, they hit pay dirt. An older model Jeep Grand Cherokee, a vehicle that took Max less than thirty seconds to hotwire.

"Your skills are starting to scare me, Max." She harrumphed.

"You know what they say, Vi: if you want something done, you send a Marine." That smirk again. He helped her into the Jeep and Blitz bounded in after her. He put the Jeep in neutral and eased out of the long driveway, checking to make sure no one was awake or on the street looking for them.

"You need to stay down until we can get out of town. Blitz will cover you, but at this hour, we don't have any traffic to blend in with, so I need you safely out of sight. OK?" he said. He'd ditched his hat and hoodie to change his silhouette.

She nodded and hunkered down, wrapping an arm around Blitz and kissing the fur at his neck while Max navigated them out of Saratoga Springs.

CHAPTER EIGHT

MAX

Vi had dozed. He was driving the speed limit to not draw attention to their vehicle, and he looped back a handful of times to ensure they weren't being followed. They were almost back to his motel room at Lake George, but he knew they couldn't stay there long. It was a matter of time before whoever was after them spread their search. Their saving grace was that this area was a tourist's wet dream and there were literally hundreds of places to stay. His name was on the hotel room though because he was supposed to just be on leave. He'd come to a place he knew Alex had loved. He'd been in town for a few weeks and had met a few of the locals while getting coffee and meals. He'd kept a low profile to grieve the loss of Alex and the others on their team, but he hadn't been trying to hide. If those assholes were smart, and he knew they were based on what he'd seen so far, they'd have his prints and registration from his truck soon. Once they had his name, it wouldn't take long to track them.

But hell, Violet needed a minute to regroup, and he needed the story of what may be going on, or they had no chance. It was time to work on what was happening and check in with Luke. He hated getting shot at, and most importantly, he was starting to realize that anyone attempting to hurt Vi was a dead man as far as he was concerned.

"Vi, babe, we're here," he said. Blitz nuzzled her throat as her eyes popped open.

"I'm so sorry, Max! I can't believe I fell asleep." Her eyes were sleepy and her voice had a little raspiness to it.

"It's OK, Vi, that's your system coming off the adrenaline rush. You've been through too much in a short time. I've got you. We're going to get inside and check in with Luke."

She took his hand, and they made their way into the small motel room, right on the water. It was small but clean and overlooked the clear lake with the rolling red, green, and golden hills as backdrop. It oozed peace in the daylight, yet the shadows and ripples of the lake gave it some mystery at night. She shivered and turned away from the window.

Blitz had been outside and was getting his dinner from Max. She crossed her arms.

"Why don't you take a hot shower, Vi? I'll get some things packed up to head out while you do that and then we can check in with Luke together, see if we can figure out what's going on."

"Yeah, OK, that actually sounds wonderful. Thanks, Max." She rubbed her arms again and crossed the little room to the bathroom. The door shut behind her with a soft click and he heard the water start in the shower-bathtub combo. He closed his eyes and sighed. She'd been through it tonight, that was for sure. And yet, she hadn't hesitated. She'd been right there with him, fighting beside him and Blitz to get to safety. She'd refused to leave him behind. She'd probably saved his life with that driving of hers.

It had been a wild night and maybe once the adrenaline wore off and they talked about what was going on, just maybe, his fascination for her would start to wane. He barely knew her and yet he felt light for the first time in months. He could breathe a little without the weight of Alex's death sitting on his chest. She just seemed to click with him. They were in sync in a way he had never experienced before. He was over his head with her already, but he knew one thing for sure, they needed to get to a more secure location and the sooner, the better.

He'd packed up what little he had, just his old seabag and then his backpack for him and Blitz. He'd need to get more treats for Blitz when he could, the dog had earned them tonight. Speaking of, the dog was passed out, back flush to the door to the bathroom. Violet might not know it, but Blitz had adopted her already.

He knocked softly on the door. "Vi? You OK?" No answer. He knocked again and gently opened the door, stepping over a deadweight dog who looked up at him with accusing eyes. "I'm just checking on her, boy, it's fine. Vi? You OK, sweetheart?"

His eyes landed on her jeans and sweatshirt folded on the little vanity top in a neat pile. It was what was on top of the pile that made his heart slow in his chest to a deeper thud. Black fucking lace. And not much of it. Hell, had she had that on all night? His mouth watered before the thought finished forming in his brain.

His eyes coasted across the steam-filled space to the sheer shower curtain. Her curves were just visible, her hands running along the dip at her back, leading to that delectable ass.

Fuck! He wasn't a creeper. He shook his head and looked down. "Vi," he said louder, "sweetheart, we should hit the road." He didn't look up, he couldn't. He didn't trust himself. He heard the water shut off. He heard her deep sigh, he felt that deep sigh. He heard the curtain pull back. "Max?" Her raspy voice scraped across him.

"We should go," he murmured without looking up. "I want to put some ground between us and whoever is after you."

"Max." Her voice was soft but strong. "Max, look at me."

"I can't, Vi. I don't think I could look away if I did."

He heard her before he felt her. And then, he smelled her fresh soap scent as her red-painted toenails stood toe-to-toe with his running shoes. "Max?"

"Vi?" He lifted his hands as if in slow motion, almost in a trance. He laid them on her hips, barely caressing her supple skin. It was hot to the touch and at the gentle squeeze she sighed against him, her arms going around his neck.

"Max, I need you to kiss me. I need you to touch me. Don't tell me it is too soon or that it's the adrenaline. I know what I want, and right now, I want you to make me feel alive. Please, I need you," she said, her voice firm.

Max considered himself a strong man. He'd done three tours in Afghanistan, he'd made it to a special forces team within the Marines. He'd survived a literal hellscape trying to pull Alex from the flames of a bombed safe house. He'd heard his team screaming to abort mission as he dragged his brother's body out of the inferno, but that strength was nothing right now.

His arms swept around her naked frame and wrapped her into him, his hands sweeping up her back and around her neck to hold her face. He looked into her eyes, giving her one last chance to stop whatever this was.

"Sweetheart, be sure. I am not feeling casual about you or whatever this is."

Her eyes fluttered and she closed the distance to his lips. Her lips sparked a madness inside of him, he felt feverish with devouring her mouth. Her moans deepened and her fingers tightened in his hair. His left hand skated down her bare back, across her ass. He palmed her tightly to his core, moaning himself as she nibbled along his jaw. Her breasts arched into him, and his right hand breezed around her nipple. He gently rolled it between his fingers, drinking in her sharp gasp as she kissed him again. Her tongue swept against his and his hand continued that delicious torture. Her hands had dropped to his hips with her small fingers coasting under his shirt across his chest. She dragged her pointer finger along his abs as he dipped his head down to pop one of her rosy nipples into his mouth. The blood had drained from his head to his aching cock in seconds. His only thought was to possess her, wholly.

His long finger skimmed along her bikini line, the calluses on his finger rough against her sensitive skin.

"Max, yes. God, Max. Don't stop."

He wasn't sure he could stop. His middle finger lined her and dipped inside her heat. She was soaking for him. His breathing was ragged, and Violet was wild in his arms, her hands everywhere. He pushed in deep and curled his finger against her clit.

"Don't you dare stop, Max," she breathed into his ear. Her lips nipped his earlobe. His mouth went back to her breasts, laving them with his rough tongue. She was thrashing against him, so close to coming. He could feel the tension in her, coiling. "Come for me, baby, let go. I've got you. Right there, baby, feel how wet you are for me."

"Max!" She came undone. She shook lightly against him as he kissed her lips and kept his finger on her, gently soothing the wetness of her along her own skin, keeping his finger against her humming clit. She whimpered against his mouth and threaded her fingers into his hair again, running along his scalp. She arched against him, so wet and so ready. He was drowning in her. His mind reverberated with "mine," just as his phone trilled from the nightstand. He ignored the ringing, lost in the feel of her. Her warm, soft skin under his hands, those little pants and moans in his ear, those lips, the wetness drenching his hand.

The phone trilled again, and this time, Blitz whined. Shit. He'd never been that lost in a woman before. She was like a drug to him. He brought his hands back to her hips and stepped back ever so slightly. He leaned his forehead to hers and kissed her again before stepping back fully. He tipped her chin up, made sure she saw his eyes and the possession there.

"Whatever that was, we will be doing more as soon as possible."

She dropped her head and giggled against his chest. "Yes, please."

He stepped to the phone, Blitz now awake and by the door again. He took a deep breath and tried to clear the lust from his overheating body. "Luke, we're back in Lake George, but I had to ditch my truck. I need an alternate plan, and soon. Those assholes know what they're doing."

"Max, Brandon was already dead. Someone got to him before we could save him."

Max's eyes met Violet's in the bathroom mirror. She couldn't hear what Luke had said. She gave a soft smile and started getting dressed, her movements languid and sated. He looked down again and willed his brain to focus.

"And, buddy, Brandon was Brandon Mills, the only son of the Speaker of the House of the United States of America."

Luke's call had been just the bucket of cold water he needed.

CHAPTER NINE

VIOLET

They were in the Jeep again, heading east, Max's hand holding hers on the console and Blitz snoring in the back seat. Her limbs were heavy and her heart calm. This man. This man she had known for less than half a day had just given her the most intense orgasm of her life. While she was on the run. While Brandon lay dead in a hospital. And she knew, without a shadow of doubt, that they were coming for her next.

Brandon had been awake and alert after the accident. She had spoken to him. He had told her, repeatedly, to go back to the hotel. The hotel she was almost ambushed at. But was he trying to save her? He didn't seem surprised by the "drunk" driver hitting them. He seemed more angry or annoyed than surprised, but had she read him wrong? She didn't really know him either.

Two new men in her life in the span of the last twelve hours and one was dead, and the other had already ingrained himself into her very being. What was happening to her? She should probably feel embarrassed that she'd come on to Max, but she couldn't find it in her to feel that emotion in regard to what had happened in that little hotel room. This behavior was so far out of the norm for her, but it all felt so natural. She had needed to feel him, for him to make her feel safe. He'd done that and more. Her hand tightened in his, making him glance at her again.

"Are you OK, babe?" He was worried about her, and maybe

worried how she felt about how big their feelings seemed to have gotten so quickly.

"I'm OK. I just can't believe he is gone. I mean, I didn't know him at all really, but he was a nice guy. I think he may have even been telling me to go, like he was trying to get me to safety from something, but I don't know why I feel like that. Does that seem crazy?"

She watched his face while she talked. He heard her and he paused to think about it before responding. "Tell me everything, why do you feel that way?"

No brush-off, just trust in her gut and the need to know more to protect her. This guy. She could see him being everything to her very quickly. She braced herself and told him about the exchange while Brandon was being put into the ambulance. She detailed how he looked, how the EMTs didn't seem urgent, like everything was a precaution, but how he was adamant she get back to the hotel.

"So, he was either sending me to danger or trying to send me to safety. Or he knew nothing and we are back to square one."

"Did you know his dad is the Speaker of the House?" Max asked,

"I did. I'm a journalist in DC. I just thought I was getting to attend a very fancy party at a cool historical site, which would be good inspiration for the novel I want to write. Brandon was a blind date, but I googled the hell out of him before I actually agreed," she said sheepishly.

"Smart girl." His praise warmed her.

Max's phone rang again before he could say more. "Luke, tell me you have an alternate plan."

Luke had arranged for them to stay in a place outside of Little Compton in Rhode Island. It was off the grid while being as high tech inside as possible. Perimeter sensors, alarm systems fortifying every water-front inch, rocky cliffs, and two escape paths if they were located.

"How do you come up with these places, man?" Max asked gratefully.

"A fraternity brother, and the less you know, the better." Luke chuckled. "The important thing is that you'll be safe there while we work to identify all the players in this puzzle. You guys hunker while we try to figure out what the actual fuck is happening. And, Vi, I know you can hear me on speakerphone. Hazel is safe but you can't call her. I'm covering her. Trust Max to cover you and we'll talk again once you guys get there. I need to follow a lead on our departed friend Brandon, and then we are going to sit down and talk this through."

Violet's cheeks heated when her first thought about Max covering her was R-rated. Yes, indeed. She was game for that, even if her cheeks were scorching right now.

"Luke, thank you." She cleared her throat again. "Truly, Luke, I'd be dead without you, Max, and Blitz. Please, keep Hazel safe."

"Ah shit, Vi, you know I love ya like the little sister I never had. Take care of my grumpy-ass friend, his cool dog, and try not to get yourself killed while I find out what our friend Brandon was into. And, Vi, Hazel will be safe, I promise you." With another "Later, brother" to Max, Luke rang off.

The final couple of hours over to Little Compton were uneventful with only a stop in Tiverton at a little place called Groundswell. Violet was in awe of this little nook of Rhode Island. It was a little grocer, cafe, gift shop, coffee shop and she wanted to stay there forever. It felt warm and cozy and solid. Judging by Blitz's tail wags, he was also a big fan. The stop had lent a vacation feel for them all, even though they were almost literally running for their lives.

Max loaded them up on gooey sticky buns and hot coffee and they ate in little blue-and-white French chairs overlooking the gardens. They'd been the first customers as the place opened, steam rising from the coffee and the delicious smells of fresh baked goods all around them.

Violet could close her eyes and picture that this was happening in an alternate universe. One where this was a normal date with a handsome man she'd just met, with his dog joining them. The problem with that was that she did feel like she already knew him far better than a first date. He was kind, he listened to her, and had shown that he always put her first in the crazy hours of their getaway. She watched him lick the residual sticky caramel off his thumb, his tongue sweeping out to catch it innocuously. Her core clenched and she looked down before he saw her blush. What was it about this man? She felt tied to him so deeply, so quickly, and yet she was also in the throes of the newness of learning another person. His little quirks, the way his smile shifted up on the side and the lines around his eyes crinkled when he smiled to reassure her. When he spoke—that deep voice rumbling across her, making her belly tighten—she shook her head to focus.

"I'll get us some food here for the rest of today and tomorrow and then let's get out to the house. I'll get you settled in and then go for more long-term provisions if it feels safe enough to leave you there for a few minutes. Luke assured me that the house is outside of Little Compton enough that we can access what we need but secluded enough that we will have lots of privacy and clear line of sight for about a mile in every direction. We should only have another thirty minutes or so, depending on the morning traffic on these two-lane roads."

"That sounds good. I'll help you grab stuff here and we can hit the road," she replied.

They cleaned up their table and walked back inside Groundswell. Max grabbed them a basket and added a few loaves of puffy focaccia, meats, cheeses, and pints of salads and roasted veggies. Violet popped some scones and cookies on top, two bags of the specially roasted coffee, and then wandered off to look at the gourmet dog treats for Blitz. She noticed Max's eyes tracking her and Blitz shadowing her every move. "Your turn, bud, let's get you stocked up."

She circled back to Max, placing the treats in the basket on his arm. "What are these for?" she asked Max, lifting out a little bouquet of asters, the rich purple blooms tied with a simple string.

He shifted against her, his breath hot on her ear, his lips just barely moving. "I've felt you come on my hand, Vi, this may not be a date, but you sure as hell deserve flowers whenever I can get them."

Done. She was done. This man. This dog. Minus the killers, this was a happiness that bubbled up in her throat like little fizzles from great champagne. Her eyes felt hot. He nuzzled her side, dropping the briefest hint of a kiss at the edge of her neck before placing their basket on the counter and getting cash out to pay the woman behind the register.

CHAPTER TEN

MAX

The house Luke had sent them to was definitely secluded. Secluded in that way that the very rich could be while still being part of the community. It sat a few miles out of Little Compton proper, overlooking the ocean with waves breaking against the shoreline. He could spot a couple of late-morning surfers trying to get in a few more rides and a handful of sailboats bobbing farther out in the water. As soon as they entered the drive, an alert popped up on his phone. Pulling it out to check it, he was relieved to find that it was the live feed of the perimeter, showing him their very own Jeep approaching. He had entered the code Luke gave him on the gate and was grateful that Luke already had him tied into the system. Once he got Vi settled inside, he was still going to set up his own system and check this out for weak spots but he knew Luke. This spot was the perfect place to figure out what they were dealing with. He wanted Violet free of this danger and he would do anything he could to make it happen.

The house itself wasn't huge, more like a luxury, two-story cottage with cedar shingles graying from the salt spray, and wide windows overlooking the water from every available angle. Inside, there were three bedrooms on the main floor, a wide living room lined with bookshelves, a fireplace, and that gorgeous view. The walls were a soft white everywhere with the furniture in muted blues and greens. The kitchen opened to the living room with a breakfast nook facing the beach.

Wide wooden beams overhead warmed the space so that the white cabinetry and marble counters didn't seem too cold.

The primary suite had the same creamy walls with a bleached wood, canopy-style bed, complete with rich green linens. It also had a fireplace and killer views of the ocean. The blinds were remote-controlled and open now, showing off the late-morning sun. Inside the adjoining bathroom, he heard Violet exclaim over the claw-footed tub. When he peeked inside, he found her sitting, fully clothed, looking as small as a child in the giant space. "Max, check this out! This thing is huge! We could both fit in here at the same time!"

Scarlet flamed through her cheeks and across her neck as soon as the words were out. He chuckled and shifted to hide his growing erection. "Yeah, um," he cleared his throat, "we definitely could. Should. Could." He chuckled again as she jumped out.

"Should is the right word, Max." Something about this man made her practically brazen. She leaned into him, her arms skating around his middle, her head resting against his chest. The hug was both so simple and so evocative of the deeper connection already forming for both of them. He squeezed his arms around her briefly as they both pulled back.

Max knew they needed to get started on figuring out the puzzle Violet had stumbled upon, or they could never truly be safe. They had a check-in call with Luke soon and he knew they couldn't miss that without Luke coming in hot. He kissed the top of her head as they both let their arms drop. "Soon, sweetheart. As soon as I have you safe, we're trying out that bathtub."

The call with Luke rang out across the kitchen, the speakerphone engaged so that they could both talk freely with Luke.

Violet walked them through the last few weeks of her life, finishing up articles at *Constitution Now*, details about those articles, which were all fluff pieces. There were a few threads there to pull, yet nothing stood out blatantly. Without access to her computer, she couldn't be certain there weren't details she was forgetting, so she really needed to get her hands on her back-up storage space in the cloud.

"Tell me about the party at the Saratoga Springs battlefield, Vi. How did that come to be?" Max asked.

"It was a blind date, set up by my boss. He knows, I guess, knew Brandon's parents through some old college connection. I had taken time off to try and start a novel and was looking for a place to feel inspired. When I mentioned maybe going up to the Springs, my boss told me about the event. Of course, there was no way I could get into that fundraiser on my own, yet he pulled some strings and connected me with Brandon. I never even met him before last night. We texted about details. I borrowed a dress from a friend and packed it along in my bag. I got in later in the day on Wednesday, woke up early, and hiked the park yesterday morning and then came back to the hotel to have lunch, rest, and get ready. Brandon picked me up and we went up to the park. It was all very surface level. He seemed like a nice guy. The party had a formal dinner on the grassy expanse next to the visitor center and then the drinks and dancing were set up on the patio on the back of the center, overlooking the battle site and valley."

"It was a really beautiful night. Not necessarily my crowd, but the atmosphere felt charmed. I only spent one-on-one time with Brandon while eating at the larger tables, and even then, there were other people around. We didn't talk about anything specifically. Where we did our respective undergrads, siblings, weather, that type of stuff. I don't even remember if we got much past those basic topics, it was all very mundane." She shrugged her shoulders and looked back at Max. She felt like such a failure at the moment. Clearly, she'd found trouble somewhere, but she couldn't put her finger on anything that stood out.

Max's hand snaked to the back of her neck, the calluses rough against the skin under her hair. He gave a gentle squeeze.

"It's OK, Vi, we'll figure this out."

She flashed him a small smile. "Thanks Max." She was glad Luke wasn't in the room with them. It felt like a tiny moment of privacy, and she didn't want to share those yet.

"I haven't seen any photos from the event, Vi, tell us more about the crowd and the cause. Maybe there is something there," Luke's voice came over the speakerphone.

"The fundraiser could have been in any DC ballroom, the crowd was identical. It was a who's who and nepotism delight. You know about Brandon's dad, and I also saw three senators, a few ambassadors, higher-ranking White House officials, pretty much the melting pot of DC elite. I briefly met Ambassador Neil, but truly, that was but for a moment right before we left." She pursed her lips again. "But wait, you won't see photos online, Luke, it was to be a cell phone-free event. In fact, people were supposed to check in their cell phones when we arrived. I remember because I actually forgot to check mine in. I'd had it off from earlier in the day and had forgotten to plug it back in. When they checked bags, it was in my wristlet, but that was so small and matched my dress, they didn't even check it. Brandon waltzed us through that part and I felt very VIP. It wasn't until after dinner that I even remembered I had my phone with me. I had stepped inside to use the restroom and was touching up my lipstick when I felt it in my wristlet. I didn't get it out and didn't really think about it again until right before we left." Here, she paused and looked contrite a bit as Max studied her, maybe even a little shy.

"Actually, right before we left, I powered it on and took a quick snap of the party in full swing and a quick flash of myself to prove to Hazel that I'd actually gone through with the blind date and the full nine yards of makeup, hair, and dress. I tried to send it to her, but it wouldn't go through, so I saved it to send to her later, turned the phone back off to conserve the battery, as it was almost dead. Then, I put my phone back in my wristlet." She paused.

"After that, I told Brandon I was ready to leave, and we left. We didn't talk much in the car and then the accident happened. Was that just last night? I can't believe all that has happened since then and I am racking my brain to figure out what is happening. Do you guys think it is related to the party?" She asked.

There was a beat of silence from the phone and from Max. Max met her eyes, and his hand covered hers on the cool marble countertop.

"Vi, this is good. This is a good start. I think it's clear that the accident was intentional, we just need to figure out why and who all was involved. I'll be direct, it doesn't look good that Brandon has since died at the hospital. It's too neat. Nothing is that neat with humans involved." Max's eyes met hers, direct and honest.

"Let's get you a computer and see what we can learn. Luke, will you take care of that? I can go back into town and get provisions for us and pick that up." Max spoke into the phone.

"I'm on it, man. I'll have something ready in two hours and will send you the details of where to get it. Once you pick everything up and get back to the house, I'll send you instructions and have Mila walk you through a secure site to start digging."

Max knew Mila, their CIA tech contact, from his special forces days. She was the best tech person he had met, and he knew he could trust her. "Off the books, right?" He asked Luke just to be clear he wasn't taking any chances with Vi's safety, whether he knew and liked Mila or not.

"Actually, very off the books. Mila's good for it." Luke gave an uncharacteristic cough to clear his throat. "Mila has actually been helping me create a fake online footprint for Hazel over the last twenty-four hours. She'll help us and can do it without anyone knowing, but we'll be secure and clean online," Luke replied.

Max saw Violet's shoulders lower again, and she sighed

deeply. "OK, Luke, I'll dig in as soon as I can. Until then, I'll start writing notes on paper about details from the last month to get my memory flowing," she said.

"Luke?" Max asked.

"Ya, man?" Luke responded.

"You can tell Hazel that Violet did the whole nine yards with the gown, the hair, and the makeup and was the most stunning woman I have ever seen doing it." Max smiled at Violet and clicked the end button on his phone while Luke laughed in the background.

CHAPTER ELEVEN

VIOLET

She explored the house while Max was gone. He had assured her that it was safe, or he'd never leave, and she trusted him. She'd seen him from the windows hiking the perimeter and checking the alerts that pinged his phone. Blitz had stayed with her and hadn't left her side.

She had wandered upstairs and found the entire second story to be one large, open space with some nooks and crannies for reading, wave watching, or working. The fireplace had continued on up here as well and she found a desk next to it, positioned to watch out of the windows toward the lighthouse. She watched the boats in the distance and wondered for the millionth time how she had come to find herself in this place, living this life. She'd been tired of her life in DC, always writing the political PR pieces, knowing it was all crap. She had wanted to be a writer for as long as she could remember, as had Hazel. The sisters had always talked about their shared passion, yet both had wanted to go in different directions with their respective journalism degrees. She wondered how Hazel was and *where* Hazel was. She trusted Luke, so she wasn't necessarily worried but she was curious.

The girls had grown up with Luke down in rural Virginia. He'd been the slightly older brother figure. They'd been thick as thieves within their small hometown from as early on as she could remember. Their moms had become best friends and they shared so many years of playing together, then sneaking out together, family barbecues, you name it.

Then, when Luke was a sophomore, his mom had died. She'd suffered an aneurysm and died immediately while working in her garden. From that moment on, their family had changed irrevocably. Luke's dad hadn't been able to stay in their home without her and had decided to move practically immediately. He purchased a condo in DC and was ready to whisk Luke away from everything he had ever known before anyone could blink.

Thankfully, her parents had offered to keep Luke at their house until he graduated so he didn't have to change schools. In hindsight, Violet wondered if that hadn't been harder on Luke in the long run since it had been as if he'd lost both his mom and dad, practically at once. She'd have to remember to ask him someday if she ever got out of this mess. Luke had joined the Marines before he even walked across their graduation stage and the three of them had kept in touch since then. All through their respective college experiences and holidays, they'd been like real siblings. For forever, it had been the three of them, and sometimes during the holidays or when Luke was on leave during his service, they'd all be "home" at Violet's parents' house together. Recently, her parents had decided to sell the house and move to Pensacola Beach, Florida. Her mom was ready for the ease of a condo, her dad was ready for warmer winters, and they were both ready for the beach life. She worried her lip, hoping Luke had eyes on them too. She'd ask Max when he returned to confirm that. She assumed that Luke would if he was with Hazel. Luke loved their parents like they were his own. She knew he would protect them, but she'd feel better if she heard him say that they were covered.

She sat down at the desk overlooking the water and grabbed the pen and paper she found in the top drawer. She started making lists. She listed out her recent articles for the paper, the guests she saw at the fundraiser, the list of people who may have known she had a blind date with Brandon.

The words and lists started flowing, and before long, she realized that she'd filled up the entire notebook with lists. She'd written several pages of details about Saratoga Springs and the battle sites, the event, the hiking, the people. She'd added some notes about historical references and research notes she'd made before she traveled.

She was just starting to list out the day of the event in sequential order when she saw Blitz stick his head up, ears perked to a noise she hadn't even heard. Her heart started to gallop. Had she been found?

Blitz didn't bark though, and he didn't whine. In fact, he gave a little tail wag and laid his head back down on his front paws, eyes shining up at her as if to say, "My dad's back."

Violet made her way over to the windows facing the drive, seeing Max returning and pulling into the garage adjacent to the house. She finally heard the door open inside.

"Vi? Sweetheart?" he yelled through the cottage.

"Up here!" she yelled back. She came down the stairs to see him carrying the last of the bags of groceries in. He'd placed a new laptop on the counter, a new MacBook Air. "Ohhhh, I like!" she exclaimed as she opened the box to reveal the new machine in "midnight," a deep blue color. She grabbed the charger and plugged it in on the kitchen counter while he unloaded groceries and stocked the refrigerator.

"My phone is dead, too, or probably is. Luke told me to power it back down, and I haven't turned it on since then, since before you found me in the cleaning supply closet."

"Let's leave it off for now. I'm going to make us some lunch while that charges a bit and then we can call Mila to get us started. She'll know the most secure way to start digging without tipping off anyone who may be monitoring your online footprint to your location."

"Sounds good to me. Let me help you with that," she replied as he set some berries out on the counter.

Together, they washed fruit and made simple sandwiches

with some of the items they'd picked up at Groundswell. It was simple and delicious, and they talked about anything and everything.

She told him about how she knew Luke, which he had the basis of from Luke already. Luke had always talked about his "sisters" to the guys on his team. She told him about going to Georgetown, her job at the paper, her frustrations with the current, soulless writing taking up her time. He seemed to understand how draining that could feel and listened intently, peppering in questions here and there about her life.

She told him about all of the trips she'd grown up taking with her family, the older SUV loaded down with coolers, maps out, how her parents would make the girls help navigate. The books they'd swap back and forth amongst themselves. She and Hazel were both voracious readers. Give her a spicy romance or a mystery any day. Hazel liked dark romance, and when they'd swap those, Hazel would laugh at her and pretend she didn't know Violet loved those too. She blushed thinking about that and glossed over that book swapping, instead focusing on great books they'd read as kids.

"Wait, so you were actually jealous of the Box Car Children?" He laughed.

"Hell yes, Max! They feasted on blueberries and kept milk cold in streams, that's the life," she responded.

The conversation flowed so easily between them. She felt like she'd known him forever and yet was excited to know everything about him. He shared more about his childhood and what it was like having a single mom. He told her about Alex, his younger brother by nineteen months, and what he had been like. She saw the pain etched in his features as he talked about Alex, and she knew that had to be so hard on him.

"That last mission, the one I was knocked out on, was my fault." His quiet admission caught her off guard. Her heart pinched at the stress lines around his mouth and the pain in his eyes as he looked across the counter at her.

"The intel on that safe house had come from my informant. I met him in the market that morning and he'd been sure the high-value targets had been in that location. It all checked out. We planned to get in, get out, and be home within twenty-four hours, but it all went to shit. I'd been on overwatch, I'm a sniper. I saw the fucking blast from my watch point. I couldn't stay where I was and watch, there was no way. Luke was in my ear, he'd been at the exfil site with the helicopter waiting on us. Our three teammates ahead of Alex were already gone when I got in there. The bomb had gone off right when the three of them were in the middle part of the shitty building and it had come down on top of them. Alex was pinned in an interior doorframe but close to the back door. I got the beam off of him, but his leg was shattered and there was blood everywhere. He was alive then, telling me to abort and leave him. He knew, Vi. He knew he wouldn't make it. He had to have known too that I'd never leave him."

Max looked up at her again, the truth in his eyes. "I'd have died there with him if I could have, Vi. It should have been me anyway, not Alex." She rubbed her hand across his back in a soothing motion, sweeping across that broad expanse and never breaking eye contact.

"What happened, Max?" she whispered. How had this man made it back to her? She sent a silent prayer of thanks up for getting him out alive.

"Tad. He'd been on overwatch also, on the west side of the building, opposite me. He came after us both. 'No man left behind' is never just a motto for us. I'd dragged Alex and myself outside but barely. There was rubble and beams crashing down everywhere by then, but he dragged our asses out. We had two cars ready to exfil to the chopper and the other guys came running to load us up and get us to Luke. We started the day with twelve guys from our normal fourteen. One was stateside for his uncle's funeral, and one was puking his guts up back at the base from food poisoning the day before.

"We came home as a team of eight and it's my fault, Vi. It was my bad intel and I cost my brother his life." His haunted eyes found hers again. His rough thumb caressed her cheekbone and under her eyes. She hadn't even realized she was crying, but his thumb came away wet with salty tears. She felt Blitz shift away from her and into Max's legs as she enveloped him in her arms. She clung to him, each one holding the other for God knows how long. Time stood still and flew by. It could have been moments or hours, she wasn't sure which.

Again, the phone ringing forced them apart. She picked up his left hand from the countertop as he hit the green answer button on the screen. She kissed his palm and turned his hand over, lacing her fingers with his.

"Thank you, Vi," he mouthed to her as a woman's voice came over the line.

CHAPTER TWELVE

MAX

He couldn't believe he'd told her all that. His pain felt like a flowing faucet with her, he couldn't stop the words or worry about what she'd think of him, he just talked and talked with her. She knew his deepest pain and she'd held him through the racking memories of the worst moments of his life. Who was this woman? What did he do to deserve her and this moment? He wasn't sure but he would do anything to protect her.

"Mila. Thanks for helping us," he spoke into the speakerphone.

"Hey, Max! Luke filled me in. I'm so sorry this is happening to Violet! From what I've learned about her online, we're going to be best friends. I'm running some programs now on the names she gave you and Luke-a-licious earlier, and the bad news is that I am hitting some dead ends. The good news is that those dead ends tell me stuff too. Dead ends aren't common with my level of skills. I mean, I don't want to brag, but I'm the best, obvi, so dead ends mean people are covering tracks and doing it well." Mila rambled out, rapid-fire. He'd forgotten how fast she could talk and how much she could say in a very short time frame.

"Luke-a-licious?!" Violet cracked up beside him. "I love that for him, thanks, Mila. And nice to meet you, kinda anyway."

"Girl! You know Luke, he's all muscles and melty eyes with the sexiness. I mean, both yum and no thanks. He's been hung up on some other lucky lady for ages, and I will always be number one when I decide to hook up. Ya know?"

Vi laughed again and shook her head at Max. Mila never shied away from saying exactly what she thought. He wondered if Vi caught the part about Luke being hung up on another woman though. Had she realized that Mila meant Hazel? Shit, Luke probably hadn't even admitted that to himself, but all of the guys knew it. You weren't brothers with Luke without catching how often he talked about Hazel or how he lit up when he did. But that wasn't his story to tell just yet.

Thankfully, Mila kept talking a mile a minute and had launched into the programs she had running on those names, including Brandon's. He caught the last part of what she was saying, anger tightening his muscles and making his heart thud.

". . . already in your cloud though, bastards," Mila spit out.

"Wait, say that again, Mila," he commanded. He saw Vi's face frowning, her lips pursed in worry again.

"Someone has accessed Vi's cloud in the last six hours. They're looking for data aggressively. No worries though, my little loves, Mila is here to protect you. I set up some wormholes for them to fall into and they won't be able to see that you're also looking for something."

She went on to share how to turn on the computer and log in to a secure site. Max powered up the computer while she talked and walked through it with her while Vi watched over his shoulder.

"Et voila!" Mila had made it so that they could remotely and safely access Violet's cloud without someone else seeing their work. She had also, apparently, sent those assholes running in a million different online directions.

Her sunshine voice assured Violet through the speakerphone with one last comment. "Please, new bestie, not to worry though, I'm mad now and digging in. Nobody dead-ends me and gets away with it."

He just hoped that held while they figured out what the fuck they were looking for.

He'd taken Blitz outside for a bit and then taken a hot shower while Vi started working her way through her saved information, looking for anything she'd written that could have gotten her tangled in this mess. She had her lists and they'd agreed to review all of the notes she'd made together, step by step this afternoon.

He kept his shower brief and then checked in with Luke while Violet went to do the same. He heard the shower start as he made his way out of the primary suite and back into the kitchen to make some coffee for him and Vi. He'd been able to pick up some basic clothes for them both, including bras and underwear for her, while he'd been in town. He felt much better himself now that he'd had that hot shower and had clean clothes on. He was exhausted but knew he had a few more hours in him before he slept. Time to check in with Luke and see if he'd learned anything.

"Max, hey, man," Luke answered the phone. He sounded tense.

"You OK, bro?" Max asked him.

"These Burke sisters. They're killing me." Max heard his buddy let a deep sigh out. "The good news is that Mom and Dad Burke are good. I've got Brody covering them. They're oblivious and safe."

"So, why the deep sigh, Luke-a-licious?" Max poked his buddy.

"I take it Mila has gotten in touch. Ya, buddy, don't be jealous, I am Luke-a-licious. Other than that, it's Hazel. She does not like being kept in the dark about what might be happening. I sent Brian and Nate to cover her, and she slipped them already. That brat told them if she needed a babysitter, I had better get my babysitting ass over there. Fuck! Max, this woman makes me crazy sometimes. She needs spanked," Luke kept on.

"Dude, that's for you two to figure out. Please. I don't want to think about Vi's sister that way and I swear to all that is holy, your voice just got lower talking about spanking her. Not gonna lie, you're creeping me out."

"Right, buddy, like I can't hear the lust for Vi in your voice," Luke snorted back at him.

"Ya, about that. What if?" Max paused. Would Luke think he was good enough for Vi? He sure as fuck wasn't and he knew Luke kept telling him not to blame himself for that last mission, but what if he wanted better for his little "sister?"

"Brother, there would be nobody better for my girl than you. Just don't fuck it up. I really don't want to have to kill you when you've saved my ass a million times." Max smiled at Luke's reply.

"It's only been two days, do you think I'm crazy?" Max asked Luke. He felt crazy. Crazed about Vi and what they could be to each other.

"I've never once doubted your insanity, brother." Luke laughed. "But when you know, you know. We've seen too much shit to worry about what normal is in our lives. And, man, I know. I know without a shadow of a doubt, that not only would you die for her, you'd kill for her."

Luke was right. Max would kill for Violet. He'd do whatever it took to keep her safe.

CHAPTER THIRTEEN

VIOLET

She felt like a different woman after her hot shower and, bless him, clean underthings and clothes. She washed the La Perla in the sink with a dollop of shampoo and hung it on the handle of the glass shower door to air dry. Max had done a decent job of guessing her sizes for these things, which made her heart light. He paid attention.

She'd washed her hair and pulled it back into a high ponytail. He'd also bought her leggings and a deep V-neck T-shirt. She left the bathroom and went looking in the house for him, Blitz at her side.

She found him upstairs, two cups of steaming hot coffee by his arm on the desk.

"Vi, sweetheart, these notes are incredible. I feel like I was there. Good thinking on the sequential layout." His praise warmed her.

She joined him at the desk and sat in the chair he'd pulled up so they could share space. She took a drink of the hot coffee. "Marry me, Max." She moaned into her coffee cup. "Seriously, you are spoiling me. You might think it's sudden, but when ya know, ya know." She laughed and looked up at him.

His gaze was intent on her face. "The coffee is that good, babe?" He laughed with her.

She knew they had to get to work, but all she really wanted to do was cuddle into him and explore what was building there. She took a deep breath, relaxed her shoulders, and started to walk him through what she'd created.

"I think we can rule out anything I've written. They are feature articles masquerading as hard-hitting profiles. Please." She rolled her eyes. "My editor sends me to the politician, they control the questions, anything remotely interesting is edited out, and there you have it. There is nothing in recent weeks that even resembles actual journalism." He agreed and they continued through her lists.

They worked for hours. They'd worked through every detail of the last month of her life through the afternoon hours, through the gorgeous sunset visible from their windows, splashing the room in oranges and golds. She felt exasperated, exhausted, and frustrated. She knew there was something there, they just needed to keep after it.

Max had turned on the low lighting throughout the room when the last vestiges of the purple sky had faded to black. It was time to take a break. She needed to set the puzzle pieces down and let her mind wander.

She hopped up on the desk and put her feet in the chair she'd been cramped in most of the afternoon and evening. She leaned back on her hands and considered the room around her. The lighting was low, the lighthouse beam in the distance stealing across the room every so often.

"Max, I need a break." He looked up, his eyes tired. He straightened out in the chair, working the muscles in his shoulders to loosen them up.

"I agree on both counts. It's time to take a break, and you're right, there is nothing in the last few months of your writing that anyone would take offense to. It's stellar writing, babe, but yeah, very sunshine and roses for some very not sunshine and roses people."

She leaned over and ran her fingers through his hair. "Sunshine and roses? I like asters and coffee anyway." She sighed again.

He reached up and captured her hand in his own. Slowly,

he lowered it and, without breaking eye contact, returned the kiss to her palm like she'd done to him earlier. Her heart rate kicked up.

With his other arm, he ran his hand alongside the outside of her knee, turning her body more fully toward his own. She shimmied over until she was sitting on the desk right in front of him.

He placed his hands on the outside of her knees, sweeping up to spread heat throughout her legs. He worked them down and rubbed deeply into the knots that had formed in her calf muscles. She felt herself relax and she knew, the time was right for them. She wanted him.

"Max?" she breathed out.

"Yeah, babe?" His eyes were on his own hands, sweeping along her legs, rhythmically. His dark eyes were almost black and the heat coming from them drew her in.

"I want you. I want this. Please?" She stroked her hand across his jaw. So slowly, in a trance and unable to look away from his eyes as they raised to hers.

"Are you sure, Vi? I want you too. I want you so much, but I also want you to be sure."

She nodded to him slowly, making sure he saw that she was all in with clear eyes. "Yes, Max, please."

She saw longing and possession, and a bolt of tenderness in his eyes. He framed her face with both hands and surged up to kiss her. He didn't consume like she expected at first, he nibbled. He explored, she relaxed into it, into his lips, her hands roaming across his chest, his arms. Holy hell, the guy was built.

She felt a moan deep in her throat and then, he devoured. Her V-neck was pulled over her head and tossed, his tongue laving a path to her breast as his hands worked the leggings and underwear down her legs.

He came to the top of the bra, the last barrier to her being completely naked and splayed for him, sitting right above him on the desk, facing his hungry gaze. His tongue traced the line of the bra and then he swirled it around her nipple through the thin cotton. He sucked *hard* and she felt him release the clasp at her back. She arched into his mouth as he marked his way across her sensitive skin. His hands circled down to her hips and he sat back.

She watched him, hungry. His eyes were so dark, so intense, and fixated on her body. Nipples straining toward him, wetness gathering between her legs already. The man could kiss.

"You are divine." He locked his eyes back on her. He tore off his own shirt, right as the lighthouse beam swept across them both. The pale light skated across his cut torso, showing tattoos across his chest. She traced the numbers inked across his heart and gasped as his tongue began to climb up her legs.

His hands kneaded her thighs, rising upward in time with his mouth. She ached for him.

He kissed along her core like he had earlier with her mouth. It started with nibbles, the gentlest of tiny bites and licks until she was crazy with wanting pressure inside of her. He chuckled darkly against her when she grabbed his hair tightly. "Max!"

His tongue swept against her, he stabbed against her clit with it, and then pushed one thick, long finger inside. She shuddered against him, practically coming right then.

Her fingers were tight in his hair while he ate at her. One finger deliciously stretched her while his tongue slayed her. He curled his finger back against her G-spot. The other hand tweaked her nipple and a jolt of fire shot through her. "Baby, baby, baby," she chanted. "So good. God. Baby, so good." She was so close.

He sucked down on her clit as his finger curled inside against her G-spot and she came, all over his mouth and hand. He kept licking her through her orgasm, his finger gently coaxing the tremors from her. He painted her wetness against one nipple and then met her eyes. He lowered his head and licked across the wetness he had placed there, sucking and nipping until she thought she'd come again.

"Max, I need you inside of me. Now."

"Now, Vi. I need you too. I need to be as deep inside of you as I can get." He pulled out his wallet and set a condom on the desk next to her, tossing the wallet aside. She was glad to see that it wasn't necessarily too old to be expired, but it was old enough to know this wasn't a regular thing for him.

He kicked off his jeans and kissed her again. Their tongues twisted and his hands in her hair. She couldn't get enough of grabbing his arms. She loved how his biceps flexed in her hands, how wet he had made her, how badly she wanted him to fill her, completely.

She grabbed the condom, opened it, and rolled it down his length. He was thick and long in her hands, and she gripped him at the base and pulled back up firmly. He sighed into her mouth.

"That feels incredible," he growled against her mouth.

His own hand had found its way back to her core and was pressed against her inner walls, making her pant. He pressed his thumb into her clit and took a nipple into his mouth to worship and suck. She could feel another orgasm building within her as she stroked him.

She shifted closer to the edge of the desk as he scooted his hand under her, pulling her the rest of the way to him. He stood up fully and pressed the tip of his cock against her opening. His hands were under her, impaling her on his length in a gentle push. He stayed like that, rooted against her as he looked into her eyes.

"Mine, Vi," he promised.

It was dark and delicious. She'd never had sex like this before. She felt consumed as he began to move against her, slowly and firmly. He moved with purpose and his hands had tightened against her, digging into her cheeks.

His mouth was everywhere. Her nipples were worshipped,

her neck licked, her mouth adored. She looked down and watched as his abs rippled with the power of his thrusts into her. The lighthouse light streaked across his chest as he hit her clit.

"Come for me, Vi. Come on me." He bit down ever so slightly on her nipple, and she exploded. She was incoherent, sobbing his name, coating him in her wetness. She felt him harden even further within her and piston more deeply as he came, never slowing through the explosions set off inside both of them.

He gathered her to him, his hands came up to frame her face, and he kissed her deeply. "Violet," he sighed against her lips.

He carried her down the stairs and to the primary suite bathroom. Setting her on the counter, he disposed of the condom and turned the water on to fill the giant tub.

She wasn't sure if she could talk again. She was robbed of all reason and felt like her body was floating. She had never come twice so close together, and although she had really limited sexual experience, she knew what had just happened was special. He was special.

CHAPTER FOURTEEN

MAX

He sank Violet into the tub before setting out towels and join-ing her. He knew Blitz would bark if there was danger and there was an iPad in the bathroom connected to the security feed.

She looked tousled and gorgeous and happily satiated. If he could remember her like this forever, he'd die a happy man. He'd had lots of sex before; he wasn't a monk but not a man whore like some of his Marines brothers had been as soon as they hit the service. He had never had anything like what they'd just shared. She was perfection. He felt his cock rising in the water, ready to go again, but she had to be sore. He was a big guy and proportionate. He needed to chill the fuck out.

She'd twisted her dark hair up into a knot high on her head and was leaning against the other side of the enormous tub with her feet in his lap. He held her foot in his large hands and was rubbing it, talking through different scenarios with her about what they'd reviewed earlier.

It was always so easy with them. He felt none of the awkwardness, none of the nervousness that he would have expected to feel. The words just came easy. And good God, she was so smart. They traded ideas back and forth until the water cooled enough to be considered tepid at best. He had just thought that it was time to get out before she shivered and he felt her other tiny foot nudge him on the underside of his balls. His thumbs had been running against the arch of her other foot and he paused to dig more deeply into her sole. She moved again. She had stopped talking and was waiting on him to look up. She shifted her foot again and he almost embarrassed himself by coming like a teenager.

He met her eyes. She pulled back on both of her feet and shifted to kneel astride of his legs, one knee on each side of him. She rubbed her hands up his legs, starting at the ankles and moving up toward his now fully erect and excited cock.

She seemed to purr low in her throat as she encircled him with her hands. She used the suds to wrap and squeeze him, slowly dragging her hands up and down while never looking away. She rinsed his skin and leaned down to kiss his leaking tip.

My God, he was gone for with this woman. She was his.

He grabbed her around the waist and pulled her to him. His cock flush to her. "No more playing, Violet," he warned her.

She licked her lips. Christ. This woman. "Max?"

"Vi?" he replied as his thumbs swept along the underside of her heavy, full breasts.

"I'm clean. I mean, I've only had sex with two other guys. One in college and one a year ago, and I've never had sex without a condom, but um, I'm clean and I have an IUD. I want to feel just you." She dipped her head but held his gaze.

He hated hearing about other men and sex with her. It made him feel murderous and yet she was offering him a gift he'd never had and she'd never given. He shuddered against her, his ab muscles rippling with the force of not pushing up into her without finishing this conversation.

"Violet. You humble me. I'm clean. I had a physical four months ago and am clean, but I haven't been with anyone in over a year either." His hands covered her breasts and his hand splayed across her collarbone. He could see her pulse fluttering like wild in her neck.

She kept her eyes focused on his and sank down onto him.

One smooth motion and he was fully seated inside of her, his cock pressed tightly against her clit. She stilled and braced her hands on his chest as the water slowly settled around her hips again, impaled on Max's thick thighs. They looked at each other, a first for both of them. Together, they reveled in the feel of the other person.

She started to rock along him, her walls milking him, her eyes hot on his. His hand never left her collarbone, but it tightened and curled around the back of her neck while the other hand tugged at the tips of her hair, now falling down along her shoulders.

Her breasts were glistening and begging to be sucked. He drew one into his mouth and swirled his tongue around her nipple, kissing his way across her chest to lave attention equally. His hand tightened in her hair and she started to rock harder along his cock.

She was practically keening, "Yes, yes, yes," as she continued to ride him, dropping her head back further. He feasted on her breasts and his hand tightened to a fist, wrapping her hair around it and pulling.

She became practically incoherent, blissed out. She rocked faster and faster against him. His thick cock was running against her clit, his mouth was hot on her skin, and that tug on her hair was driving her wild. Her hips were moving on their own, and he knew she was close.

He dropped the hand that had been encircling her neck to her stomach and pushed against where he was inside of her, dropping his thumb to push down on her clit tightly. Her cries rang out in the marble bathroom and she came against him. Her sex had tightened around him, strangling his cock. Her heat felt like velvet. Her orgasm was sending ripples against his length and he felt that rushing in his spine, he was so close. She tightened on him as her orgasm drew out, shattering him. He came moments after her, his warmth shooting inside of her. Stars danced across his vision. "Violet!"

After, they lay panting together, the water around them cold. Max drained the tub and refilled it without pulling out of Violet. She felt too good, he couldn't make himself pull out of her just yet.

She was nuzzling his neck and kissing across his jaw. Her hands came up to brace his face and she whispered, "Never been like this before."

They kissed lazily, soaping each other up and rinsing each other. By unspoken agreement, they cuddled and touched but didn't take it too far. They got out of the tub and dried off. He pulled his T-shirt from earlier down over her head, giving a little spank to her cheeks before he backed away. She laughed and kissed his chest as he pulled on a pair of gray sweats.

They moved into the kitchen, and he let Blitz out to run. Blitz wouldn't run off, but he needed some time outside.

Max picked Violet up and placed her on the counter, moving around her to get ingredients out to make dinner. He'd picked up fresh fish during his shopping trip and they had roasted veggies from Groundswell, along with a loaf of crusty baguette.

He sprinkled the fish with salt and pepper and then pan sautéed it before setting it in the oven to finish. He set to work creating a sauce of lemon, a little cream, and herbs he'd found. Max knew how to cook. He'd had a single mom and a young brother and he wasn't going to rely on processed food growing up. Both boys had played multiple sports in high school, and he'd had a coach drill the need for a decent diet into his head. They may not have always had the gourmet ingredients he had today but they had always eaten well.

Vi watched him work and they talked more about her favorite books growing up. She still couldn't read *Where the Red Fern Grows* without crying, and frankly, he couldn't either. That book. It gutted him. He let Blitz back in while the sauce was simmering just so he could wash his hands and snuggle his dog.

Blitz loved the snuggles, and they agreed to never read that book again. He fed Blitz and then washed his hands again. He pulled out a bottle of white wine and added a splash to the sauce before pouring her a glass. He wouldn't drink when he and Blitz were responsible for Violet's safety, but it would go well with the dinner, and he knew she'd love a small glass.

Vi hopped down and set places at the table overlooking the water. At this time of night, it was a dark expanse, broken up only by boats lit up and anchored and other houses in the far distance. The lighthouse light circled past the rocks that he could see every so often and it felt like a perfect moment. He could get used to this. He could get used to making her dinner while she sat next to him in his T-shirt, that look of completion and utter satiation on her face.

He served dinner, killed the lighting, and turned on the fireplace to his left in the big living room. Vi had "lit" the remote-control faux candles on the table earlier and that gave the space a feeling of cozy quietness. A serenity that he didn't think he'd ever felt before.

They'd both worked up an appetite and dug into their dinners. "Oh, Max," she moaned.

"Vi, another sound like that and the only thing you'll be moaning over is my cock. Quit it, please. I can't take it," he begged her.

The corner of her smile kicked up and she laughed. She didn't moan again but she did rave about his food. They cleared the dishes and washed up before turning off the faux candles in the breakfast nook and cuddling up on the couch.

How he had managed to get through a meal with her wearing only his shirt was beyond him. Fuck, he should get a medal. He pulled her onto his lap and lightly braced his hands around her hips.

She sighed into his chest, running her hands along his arms.

"Max, if I had a camera, I'd capture you just like this. The firelight on your handsome face, the muscles in your chest—those are so hot by the way—your tattoos. You are everything. I'd capture you just like this."

He gripped her hips tighter. His heart felt light and he knew this woman was it for him.

Something she said stuck out to him though. If she had a camera . . .

"Vi! That's it! The camera!" His shout hit her consciousness and she paused, eyes alighting on him and a wide smile breaking across her face.

"OHMYGOD, Max! Yes, the snap!"

CHAPTER FIFTEEN

VIOLET

It was late, but as soon as the phone rang once, they heard, "Mila here, at your service, Bestie and Maxie." She laughed.

"Mila, we need to power up my phone. We think I accidentally captured something on video when I snuck a snap and selfie at the party. I can't find it in my cloud though. Do you think someone found it on there and already deleted it?"

"Violet Bestie Burke, how dare you! No, no one already found it on your cloud. Those dickheads are still caught in a wormhole of my choosing. You take that back right now and I'll think about forgiving you." Mila replied.

Violet laughed while Max rolled his eyes.

"Mila, why is it in her phone but not in her cloud?" Max asked.

"It's a matter of timing, Maxie Cakes, and some skill on their part. If Vi captured it and then immediately saved it and powered back down or her battery died, it probably just happened too fast. If they had a jammer at the event, which I can tell you they for sure did, whoever our dickhead 'theys' are, the snap is actually only on her phone until she turns it back on and has internet service again." Mila explained.

"But why wouldn't it have synced when I was in the hotel, Mila? It all happened really fast, but I know I had connected to the hotel Wi-Fi earlier in the day. And what about my hotspot?" Violet asked.

"This is where the skill they have comes in guys. My sense

is that they had jammed you, then when you weren't knocked out or killed when they ran you off the road, they continued to jam you, thinking they'd get the phone back at the hotel before you even realized you even had a chance to know you had captured something. They would have been worried about you sending it if you had service." Mila's voice trailed off, pensive.

"So *they* knew she captured something, they just didn't know if *she* knew she captured something. They needed to kill her to bury what she had and what she may know she saw," Max gritted out. He stood up to pace as her stomach sank.

"Right. And as soon as we connect her phone to Wi-Fi to examine the video, we risk her location being compromised and the video being deleted. I like to send the dickheads on chases, but that will only work for so long." Begrudgingly, Mila admitted what they all knew. These dickheads were good, and well-funded to have had the coverage and skill they were displaying so far.

"Hang tight, one of my programs found something." They heard Mila clicking rapid-fire. "Did you know Brandon's mom is actually not Mrs. Mills? Her name is Linda Pell and her family founded Pell Weaponry. It looks like she divorced Speaker Mills about twenty years ago but had never taken his last name during their marriage. That's why it took a bit to connect those dots."

"So, Brandon's mom's family manufactures weapons? What type?" Max asked.

"It looks like all types, and they do global distribution. You've used them before during tours. It looks like they have one of the largest contracts with the Department of Defense out there," Mila answered.

Violet's eyes met Max's, fear once again taking hold.

Based on how late it had gotten, they agreed to all get some sleep and let Mila's programs, running on Brandon and now Linda, see if they could uncover any additional data by tomorrow morning. It was late, they needed to connect Luke in, and they needed a plan.

Max disconnected the call with Mila and pulled Violet in close. He held her against him in that now-familiar hold, big hands sweeping across her back, lips along her jaw, promises breathed against the shell of her ear.

He scooped her up, his hands digging into her bare cheeks as he carried her to bed. He laid her down reverently, sliding against her.

"Rest, Vi, I've got you." She clung to him. He needed to check the perimeter again and ensure lights were out, but she needed him more at the moment. He swept his hands along her curves and murmured his promises to her until she drifted off. He felt her body uncoil and relax fully into sleep as he held her. He brushed a kiss against her forehead and eased from the bed.

He took care of Blitz and then left the dog to watch over her while he checked outside. He made quick work of it, eager to get back to her.

Once inside the dark house, he had to nudge Blitz out of bed. His dog made a sound he'd never heard before when he made him move away from Vi in the bed. Clearly, he wasn't the only one in deep with this woman.

He slid off his sweats and eased under the covers with her, pulling her back to his front. His dick took notice. How could it not? She had that perfect ass nestled against him. He willed his body to chill out, she needed sleep and so did he. It had been almost forty-eight hours since he had slept and he knew that although he was trained to do this, he was human and needed the recharge.

He kissed the back of her head and slid his land over her hip, pressing against her stomach to tighten her body to his. She wiggled ever so slightly deeper into him and he closed his eyes, letting sleep claim him.

CHAPTER SIXTEEN

VIOLET

She stretched against the cool sheets on her soft skin, the last vestiges of a delicious dream fading away in the faintly golden sunrise filtering through the windows. Her breasts were so sensitive and bare against the satin. She felt like liquid, sinuously caught between those sheets and Max's hot lips as they worked their way up the backs of her thighs. His hands were kneading her cheeks, murmured words of adoration rumbling from his throat.

"This ass, Vi." He nipped at her. "Mine."

She loved that possessive streak he displayed. She felt cherished in the reverent way he meant it. His actions were showing that he was just as much *hers* as she was *his*, and she loved it. She tilted her butt back against his mouth more firmly as he continued his nipping and licking.

His left hand snuck around to her belly and firmly worked its way down to the gathering wetness at her core.

"Baby, you kill me. Is all this for me?" He rubbed along her inner walls, and she could hear how wet he had made her.

She groaned in response as he worked those fingers lazily against her clit. Her own hand reached down and pressed against the back of his, she needed him to add pressure because he was killing her slowly.

He bit her lightly on the right cheek and rasped, "You want more, baby, take it."

He moved his hand from underneath hers and then placed

his hand on top of the back of hers as hers had been moments before. He pushed her own fingers deeper into her slick heat, her palm adding relief to her clit. He pushed her fingers until he knew she'd take over and then his hand snaked up, tweaking her nipple hard as his lips coasted up and kissed the very top of her ass. His mouth continued along her spine, kissing her and rolling her nipples between his thumb and forefinger. She pushed back against him, nearly frantic with her need to come. She'd played with herself before, but never with someone. She felt like she was about to combust. His hot lips met her ear and he growled deeply at her while his hand came up gently, yet firmly, against her throat. "Come all over those pretty fingers of yours, baby."

She detonated. Her own fingers drenched in her wetness and her ass pushed back against him as tight as she could push back. His hand swept down and before she could come down from her first orgasm, he was pushing into her from behind, pulling her up to her knees in front of him. His hands were on her hips, rough, callused fingers digging into her creamy skin. His hips were pounding into her and she felt a light spank on her ass, then his huge palm rubbing where he'd lightly smacked her. Lord, this felt so naughty and wonderful. She'd never felt sexier, more powerful.

"Harder, Max." She pushed back against him.

His rough, strong hands flew up the sides of her body, the right hand coming around to roll her nipple along his fingers and his left pulling into her hair.

"Oh God, yes. Max!" She was coming again before she finished yelling his name, but still, he didn't quit. She felt him everywhere, surrounding her.

Suddenly, she felt herself flipped over and rolled, her legs straddling Max and his cock thick and pulsing in her core. She felt slippery around him and languid. He gripped her hips and began to move her on himself. She was riding him, but he was doing all of the work. She arched her head back and then smoothed her hands along his muscled chest. She met his eyes and they shared a smile, it was too good between them. He quickened his pace, the faint light from the sunrise casting on him a golden glow.

"Vi, I could watch you riding my cock all day, baby. So beautiful." Max lovingly moved one hand up to her collarbone and swept down the center of her chest between her aching breasts. Her breath caught as the slowly building inferno threatened to overtake her.

He pressed against her clit and came, his orgasm causing her third. He slowed his punishing pace of her hips and she collapsed against him, sweat making her hair stick to her nape and forehead.

She kissed along his collarbone, turnabout being fair play. She loved that he always focused on that zone for her and knew it felt good for him; she felt his chest groan against her own body. She nipped at him and he laughed, lightly slapping her ass again before both of his palms gathered her cheeks and pushed more deeply into her, making them both moan before he rolled them again. He feathered a kiss against her lips. "Morning, gorgeous."

She kissed him back as he slid out of her and the bed and made his way to the shower. She turned back over as he stepped inside and stretched her well-loved body deeper into the tangled sheets. She was in so deep for Max.

CHAPTER SEVENTEEN

MAX

Violet was in the shower, and it was taking herculean effort and his many years of torture training not to join her there. But Blitz needed out and they needed to start extricating themselves from this danger. He wanted her free and clear so that they could see where this was going between them. He knew he was all in but he wanted her free to choose without the constant threat of death stalking them.

He got some coffee ready and diced up some fruit. She came into the kitchen and snuck her arms around him from behind, her hands wrapping around his waist.

"MMMMM, Max, coffee and an ocean sunrise, a girl could get used to this." He smiled and turned, bringing them front to front, wrapping her in his arms too, bringing her flush to his very needy body.

"I'm a lucky man, Vi. You make me feel alive again, sweetheart." He said it directly, his eyes clear on hers. Her heart turned over.

The compliment warmed her but more so the directness of it. He wasn't coy, he wasn't playing games with her, he was just himself. He cared for her already and he showed her.

"Vi, you're a keeper." He hugged her close.

"Max! That's it! A keeper is what Ambassador Neil called me. Now I think I know what happened the night of the party, we need to call Mila and Luke."

They called Luke and Mila so they could hear what Violet

had remembered. His woman was so fucking smart. His woman, geez he was gone for her.

"Right after the snap that never sent, I made my way over to Brandon and Ambassador Neil, who had been talking quietly alone together. I didn't think anything of it at the time, but looking back, Ambassador Neil was overly loud and effusive when Brandon noticed me and introduced me. Ambassador Neil called me a 'keeper' because I knew some random facts about the battle site. He had a great-great-great-something or other there. He asked if I had been enjoying myself and I shared that I had taken a quick video. I didn't say anything after that because Brandon ended the conversation and hustled me out of there after that.

"I didn't complain because I had been ready to go and had specifically walked over to ask him if it was OK if we left." She finished her story and met Max's eyes as he smiled reassuringly. He was damn impressed with her but he didn't like where this was going. Both Brandon and Ambassador Neil were very well connected.

"And now Brandon is dead," Luke intoned from the speakerphone.

"A loose end," Mila trailed off.

They were all silent a beat, knowing that whatever Vi had on that saved snap had made her a loose end too.

"We can dig into this, Vi. Now that we know Ambassador Neil and Brandon were both involved, I can adjust my algorithm and see where to start picking," Mila said.

"If we can get more information on what this may be about while you two lay low for a few more days, we can switch to offense on this. We don't necessarily need to expose Vi's location by switching on her phone to view the video just yet."

"Right, and with Mila's help on the dark web, I can start digging into intel on my channels," Max went on. He knew he could do it, he knew he was one of the best at finding those little details, at uncovering things people tried to bury. Alex's face flashed in his memory and his heart squeezed, but for once, he didn't feel like a failure, he felt like he could help the woman he was very quickly falling for.

"I can start following money on my end," said Luke. "It all comes back to money."

They all agreed to check back in if they learned anything of value, and if they didn't hear from one another, they'd talk again the next morning.

Max and Violet worked side by side most of the day, him sharing deep search methods and her asking questions from her innate point of curiosity. Her journalist lens was great for considering threads and his methods were great for pulling on those threads.

Late in the day, Max stood up and stretched.

"Vi, we need to plan for them to find us once we turn on that phone," he said, extending his hand down to her to help her up from where she was sitting against the couch.

"Right, but what if we don't need that?"

Hopefully, they'd figure out enough of the puzzle that they didn't need to analyze the video. They didn't even know if once they watched the video, it would tell them something obvious or if it would need to be studied. They had these big chunks of the puzzle but not enough to make the whole picture clear. It felt like they were still trying to find all of the edge pieces.

"Vi, I'm taking zero chances with your safety. Zero. We are all working on this, and I know we can get more clarity, but we have to have an alternate and a contingency plan." He squeezed her hand reassuringly.

"Overkill much there, Max?" She laughed.

"With your safety? Hell no. C'mon, let's go."

The weather had shifted along the coast. It was late September in New England and the spray off the water was brisk. She grabbed a sweatshirt while Max checked their security feeds down by the beach. From the house, you could see the massive chunks of granite and the water out below, churning and frothing along the coast. She shivered.

Outside the French doors, she joined Max and Blitz and they set off toward the edge of the manicured yard toward the granite boulders. Max grabbed her hand and helped her over the smaller rocks while Blitz scampered ahead. It was like the dog had been waiting for this the entire time they'd been there. Finally!

"Where are we going?" she asked.

"I want to show you a path down to one of the contingency plans Luke set up. There is a boat down here, but you don't see the path from the house. You have to follow it down." He pulled her around one of the rock formations. "And then head down. It's a hidden path, and the boat is protected by the overhang we are working our way down from now. I've checked it over while doing my sweeps and it is truly hidden from people who don't know to look for it." He held tightly to her as they navigated between the boulders, picking their way carefully down over the wet surfaces.

The wind had whipped the sea spray all around them, but with the size of the granite chunks along this little inlet towering over their heads, they were protected. He slowed as they neared the water and then guided her around another rock outcropping, arriving at a slip with a boat in what felt like a giant mouth. The water was calm where the boat was and it was much darker.

"So, we have our own bat cave?" She laughed.

"Kind of, yeah. Remind me to ask Luke more about this fraternity brother of his who loaned us the house." He grinned at her. They turned toward the boat, which looked more "yacht-y" to her. It was certainly the nicest boat she had ever seen.

He helped her onto the deck and gave her a tour. On the bridge, he showed her the controls, how to power on, how to get out quickly. How to call for help. They went over everything enough times that she knew she could do it if she needed to, she just hoped she never needed to.

"Vi, this is the important step. I'm programming the GPS coordinates to get you to Narragansett from here. Stick as close to the shore as you feel safe doing, but let the boat get you there. Luke and I agreed that was the safest place to come back ashore as it is quicker via water than on land. If anyone is after you on land, it will take them much longer to get there than it will take you via water. If they pursue on the water, shoot them." He showed her the emergency flares. "Aim right at their boat, not up. You'll need to disable them before you call for help."

"Won't you be with me?" she asked, panic rising.

"I hope so, but we need to plan for the alternate just in case," he replied. "One more thing, Batman also carries weapons, so let's go over those. I want you to be able to protect yourself." He tried to lighten her mood. He needed her to know this alternate plan, he had to be assured she could get away safely alone if she had to.

"Here." He showed her the gun hidden inside the sleek teak of the controls. "You have flares to shoot at the boat, a gun to shoot at the assholes, and the knife if anyone gets too close." He picked up her hand and squeezed.

"You good?" he asked.

"No, Max, not good. I don't intend to do this myself. You had better be with me if we are fleeing some assholery." She looked up at him. "You have to be with me. I can't imagine leaving this place without you." Her eyes were wide and pleading.

"It's just an alternate plan, Vi, it's OK. I intend to be with you too, but I won't turn on the phone without knowing you know how to get away on your own if you have to."

He turned her away from the wall of windows and screens and pulled her into his lap, sinking down into the captain's chair. She settled against his chest, her hands running along his arms, his hands warming her back. "OK, Max," she breathed.

She shimmied in the seat, facing him, astride his lap. She glanced around at the almost 360-degree view of the bat cave and the inlet. They were sheltered in here with the sun dipping low into the horizon. Without saying a word, she unbuttoned the top three buttons of his Henley, placing gentle kisses on his skin as she went.

His hands fell to loosely rest on her hips, his thumbs circling her sides. She continued to scoot lower, crouching at his waist level, eyes never leaving his. She began to unbutton his jeans. He shimmied just enough to lift for her to pull them down, along with the black boxer briefs he had on. She licked her lips tentatively and he groaned.

Her hands ran back up the tops of his thighs, her nails dragging ever so lightly. She licked the tip of his cock, a little tease. He shuddered and she felt his hand curl into her hair. She opened her mouth wider, licking him from the base to the tip and circling around the sensitive skin. He was big, hard, but the skin was satiny against her tongue. She pulled him all the way into her mouth, her right hand coming to the base of him and pumping into her mouth. Her left hand dipped in closer and gently cradled the rest of him.

His other hand warmed the back of her neck. His hold was firm, but he didn't push. She hollowed out her cheeks, sucking him in deeply to her mouth, working him with her hand. She hummed against him, he felt incredible in her mouth. This man. This strong, protective man was coming undone for her. She felt wetness gathering between her legs. He made her feel so sexy, and she loved that she was eliciting these deep growls from him.

"Vi, I'm going to come and I want it to be inside of you." He shuddered again and met her eyes.

She kept going, sucking a little harder, her hand moving faster and firmly. His hands left her head and slid down to her waist. With a pop, he pulled her off his cock and brought her mouth to his. His tongue swept inside, and she circled her arms around him.

He pulled her back and grabbed the bottom of her sweat-shirt and T-shirt, yanking both off her. "No bra today? If I had known that, we wouldn't have gotten anything done." He suckled a breast deep into his mouth.

His hands worked her leggings down her legs, pulling them off. Seeing she also dressed without underwear, he growled at her again and switched to her other breast. Her hands dug into his dark hair.

Bracing her hips, he stood up and sat her at the controls. He paused and took her in, naked with the windows behind her. Her skin gleamed in the golden light of the sun across the water, her hair pulled down around her shoulders. Her lips were puffy from their assault on his dick. Her breasts slowing swayed with the motion of the boat in the water.

"I have never seen a more beautiful sight, Vi." He returned to her, his huge hands pulling her against him. His fingers dug into her cheeks while he devoured her mouth. Her sensitized breasts scraped across his chest. She sighed into his mouth, circling her hands across his broad shoulders.

He plunged into her, one motion and he was completely buried within her. She cried out in ecstasy, her wetness all around him. Every time felt like the most incredible feeling.

He began to move within her, laying her back onto the now off screens. He ran his hands along her arms and braced them behind her, placing them on the windows and holding them there while his hips rocked into her.

He was slow and steady, his hips thrusting with the slow rocking of the boat. His mouth nibbled a path across her chest, dragging across her breasts with his rough tongue.

Their hands were joined, fingers interlocked above her head. Her legs were tight around his lean hips, her head fall-ing back.

She was blinded with need, the slow build had created a tsunami inside of her, and she came apart, splintering into a million pieces against this man who seemed to know her very soul.

His hands swept down to her hips, lowering her arms around his neck. She arched into him and breathed out against his ear, "Max."

He came. His hips shot into her, his fingers digging into her hips and low back. He shuddered and moaned her name.

There were no words. They stayed locked together as long as possible in the setting golden light reflected off the water, each sated and kissing the other.

CHAPTER EIGHTEEN

VIOLET

They'd made love. He had worshipped her body, his kisses promising things he didn't need words for, his body connected to her in a way she hadn't dreamt possible. He felt like an extension of her. She felt cherished and deeply tied to this man.

They re-dressed and walked back up to the house, arm in arm. She wanted to be with him for sunsets and sunrises when they weren't hunkered down and hunted. For the everyday normal life things, for the holidays, for all of it.

Committed to making that happen, she was eager to dig into Ambassador Neil more. She had thought him too smooth that night at the party and her mind was spinning.

Max started dinner while she brought the laptop down to the kitchen island. They talked while she started digging into the ambassador.

"Max, what did you tell me earlier about weapons and access in Iraq? There was something about the black market that keeps pinging in my brain." She looked over at him.

He tossed the kitchen towel back over his shoulder and set the wooden spoon down. Turning to face her, he leaned his hip against the counter.

"Just that most of the weapons in the world that are in asshole hands have gotten there via backdoor routes. So many times, our own guys are killed by guns manufactured here in the States. I've seen it on every tour I've been on." He grimaced.

"So, would Tunisia fit the bill for a backdoor route? I mean, Ambassador Neil has that location as a secondary home base with its ports practically open access for whatever he needs." She paused, thinking the geography through.

"Yes, once a ship is on the Mediterranean Sea, it's child's play to get into the Middle East, there are literally thousands of paths." He stirred the sauce again, thinking about where a ship could put in from Tunisia.

"So, if Ambassador Neil wanted to, he could really smuggle anything," she mused.

"If he has a port stateside, then yes, he could." Max turned back to her. "I think this is a thread to pull, Vi. You're so fucking smart."

She blushed. "Not really, he was just so smarmy, but it could make sense. He has access and he was the only person besides Brandon that knew for a fact I had taken a video. I mean, someone could have seen me do it, but he directly knew, because like an idiot, I told him myself."

"Hey, cut yourself some slack there, how could you know that the person who may have the most to lose would be one of the two people you said something to?" he challenged her.

"Do you think Brandon knew what was going on?"

"Yes. I do. And that means that either he was greasing palms on this side of a port, or the Speaker of the House is. And if that's the case, we have a way bigger problem than just Ambassador Neil."

They called Luke and Mila, walking them through their hypothesis. "Is it too simple though? It seems too easy to have guessed for it to be right." Violet asked them.

"I don't think so, bestie. You are the only person we know of who has seen Ambassador Neil and Brandon together. You're the only one who mentioned a video that might connect the two, and the only other person who knows you have a video is dead, outside of the ambassador. It wouldn't be too far-fetched to consider that Brandon was helping him. He could have done anything under the guise of his dad," Mila reasoned.

"Let's start with digging into the New York and New Jersey Port Authority. Statistically, that would be the largest and busiest port, in addition to the sheer number of politicians that have access there. We need to know who is on the port authority's board of commission, Mila, and most importantly, who they know. This feels like the thread to pull. It would only take one of those board of commission members, approved by the senator of New York, to make something like this happen if the right chain of command was in place," Max said.

"I started poking around Neil's finances while you guys were talking," Luke chimed in. "Whoa, the ambassador is doing really well. From what I can see, his grandfather actually lost their fortune during the Great Depression, but I can't see how it was rebuilt for him to maintain the lifestyle he is living today."

Max's eyes met hers, they were on to something, they both knew it.

"Shit! Mila, the accounts are shutting down on me, what's going on?!" Luke exclaimed.

"What?!" Mila yelled. "Shit, shit, shit," she muttered. "We are under cyberattack, guys, gotta bounce, back soon." She hung up.

"Max, Vi, I don't like this. Whatever is going on is big. Brace for anything, I'm going to call you back as soon as I can." Luke hung up.

Violet shut the laptop down. The mood had shifted to tense, they were on to something. They ate dinner, both distracted and thinking through different avenues of what could be happening.

"I don't like that Mila's system was breached," Max said. Blitz had come to nuzzle against Vi and she reached down to rub his ears. "Let's lay low for now and hunker, to Luke's point."

She agreed and they cleared the dishes, cleaning up the kitchen. Violet took a hot shower and Max checked their security, complete with his nightly walk outside around the house. Once he and Blitz were back in, he joined her in bed.

"I don't like this Max. I'm scared," Violet said against his chest.

"I know, babe, but I've got you," he spoke into her hair, wrapped up in her. They made love again, their bodies communicating without words their growing connection. After, they nuzzled together and drifted off, the lighthouse light flashing through the bedroom as it made its circles across the water.

CHAPTER NINETEEN

MAX

Someone was coming. The alarms he had set to the west of the property along the beach were triggered. He slid out of bed, reaching back to quickly caress Vi's shoulder.

"Vi, babe, wake up. Someone is here. Get dressed and get the bag with your phone and laptop. The knife is here." He handed the knife to his sleepy girl.

"What? Oh, OK, yeah, I'm awake." She jumped out of bed and started pulling on clothes.

Blitz whined, leaning against Max's leg tightly while he dressed and moved through the bedroom.

Max turned back and kissed Violet, pulling her against his body quickly. "Take the bag and be ready to get to the boat." He pulled away and left the room before she could protest. Blitz stayed by her side.

Fuck, there was an army coming for them. Max counted six men from the eastern perimeter of the property and silent alarms were going off all over the place. He sent an emergency alert to Luke and switched over to a remote-activated bomb device network he'd set up right outside of the property's secure perimeter. The only thing they could do now was try to get away; there were too many assholes coming to take them on by themselves.

The first explosion shook the earth, the tremble felt in the house. He had detonated in two opposite directions to discombobulate the attackers, and it looked to be working. For now.

He met Vi and Blitz against the door leading to the cliffs and "bat cave." Silently, they slid out of the house. They were sticking to shadows along the manicured expanse, trying to reach the huge rocks when shots rang out. Max pushed her in front of him toward the safety of the path and turned, standing between the house and her body, returning a spray of fire. He yelled for her to stay low, and they crouched to run while Max set off another remote-activated minibomb to the east. They could hear yelling now and see that men were inside the house.

They crept along the cliffs as silently and quickly as they could to reach the path down. Almost there! Max had just turned back to Violet when he was slammed from behind. His attacker attempted a chokehold around Max as they grappled for the upper hand. He'd knocked the gun from Max's hand before Max was able to twist away from the gun barreled into his side. She heard shots coming from all directions.

"Vi, go!" Max shouted. She hesitated. She knew the plan but she still paused. She wanted to help him. He couldn't die for her! She hesitated as the bullets peppered around them, but then moved closer and closer, inching toward his gun.

"GO!" Max roared. She reached out her trembling hand and nudged Blitz. The dog hesitated and she nudged him again. Then, in an explosion of black fur, the dog was on the attacker. She'd never heard such savage grunts from an animal before and she knew she'd done the right thing. Shots were peppering the boulders around her, but Max was still trying to shake his attacker. They were locked in a vicious dance, and other gunmen were moving closer. She saw two more making their way out of the same French doors they had just left.

It was Blitz who made the difference, latching on to the attacker's wrist and causing the attacker to howl in pain and drop his own gun. That tiny window of time was enough, it had to be!

Violet dropped to her knees and grabbed Max's gun, sliding it to him. In one smooth motion, he grabbed it from her and rolled back around to his back, shooting the attacker in the belly.

"Go, Violet!" Max whisper yelled again, pushing Blitz to her. She turned to run down the hidden granite path while Max staggered after her, shooting at the men who had breached the manicured yard. Her heart was in her throat, and she felt another small explosion rock the earth above her. She was running now, slipping against the rocks when she rounded the corner. She jumped onto the boat, Blitz right behind her but limping. The brave dog had been kicked as the attacker tore at the dog's body to save himself, but still Blitz had never let go.

Max untied the lines and followed her on, hunched over. "Vi, I'm hit, get us out of here." He reached a bloody hand back down to his side.

"Oh God, Max!" she cried, trying to go to him.

"Just get us out of here, hit open water, go!"

She scrambled to the bridge and did exactly as he'd taught her. They were just clearing their "bat cave" when shots came from above and behind them on the path.

She grabbed the flare gun and shot it back toward the opening of the path while trying to steer them clear of the rocks. She ran back to Max and helped him inside the bridge. He opened a window along the back and took the flare gun from her. He shot toward the ledge above them, pushing back their attackers. She saw one man fall dead into the water, the lighthouse shining across his burning body as he fell to the water.

"Get us to open water, Vi!" Max yelled as he took aim again. He held them off with the flares, but they'd been made. It was a matter of time before they pursued on the water too. There were too many of them for this to be amateur hour and he had no idea how their location had been found.

He needed to get them far enough ahead to lose anyone with a boat. He staggered to the controls and killed their lights. The engines were open, but they'd need to rely on the depth finders and GPS now to not ground themselves.

Max felt blood seeping through his shirt. He needed to dig the bullet out but he needed to get them further out, away from the lights of the shoreline first. His vision was dimming but he would not go down. Fuck! Blitz was whining at his side.

"It's OK, boy, you did well." He patted the dog with his non-bloody hand.

Violet was rummaging through the teak compartments when he heard her say, "Sit down, Max, now." He collapsed into the captain's chair. He fought to stay conscious, his head lolling to the side.

"God damn it, Max, don't you dare die on me!" Violet cried. She pulled his shirt away from the wound, causing the congealed blood to loosen and the flow to start again in earnest. "God damn it, Max!"

He was losing the battle to stay awake. He reached out for her, but his hand fell to his side, grasping nothing. He'd lost the battle.

CHAPTER TWENTY

VIOLET

His beautiful eyes were closed, and his face had relaxed, his body slumped against the captain's chair. She had to help him! She took off her bra and held it against the bloody mass on his side and then ripped at her shirt, shredding off the bottom of it and then wound it around his chest as tightly as she could. It wasn't great, but it was all she could do for now.

Grabbing Max's phone, she typed in the number he'd shown her earlier and pushed "call" to Luke.

"Luke! Max has been hit! We're on the boat now, heading toward Narragansett." She was shaking so hard she had a hard time holding the phone. It kept slipping from her bloodied fingers. Oh God, her hands were covered in his blood, that's why it was slipping. She tried to wipe them clean against her legs. "Please, Luke, I don't know what to do!" she wailed.

"Is he alive? Where was he hit? Are the lights on the boat off, Vi? Are you far enough away from the shore to not take fire from land and that you aren't in any scopes of light on land?" Luke barked out questions.

"I . . . I . . . I think so. Max steered us away from the shore and hit the lights before he passed out. He was hit on his side, the left side of his stomach. His breathing is really low, Luke. He's lost a lot of blood, but I did what I could to stop the flow. Luke, he has to be OK!" She was trying to stay calm. She knew she had to get them out of this but she knew she wouldn't survive losing him in this mess. Her mess. Damn it!

"Listen, Vi, we planned for this when we laid out an alternate situation. Seb is in Narragansett and will meet you at the location plugged into the system on the boat. Shit." Luke took a deep breath. "I'll tell Seb that Max is down, he'll be ready. I can't get to you in time, but Seb is one of my team guys too, he won't let you down. He won't let Max die." Luke was tense, yet his voice was firm and clear.

She agreed and hung up. Max was still out cold, but the bleeding had slowed. She washed her hands in the sink in the bridge and soaked one of the towels in cold water. She cleaned up Max's hands, arms, and face, making sure she hadn't missed any other injuries. When she got him cleaned up, she got the towel as cold as she could and added that to the makeshift Band-Aid around Max. Blitz whined up at her, eyes sad and scared as he leaned tightly to Max's leg.

"I know, boy. But now, we've got him, OK? We need to get him to help." She patted Blitz and prayed they made it to Seb.

CHAPTER TWENTY ONE

MAX

Did he die? He felt flames licking along his side and his body was burning. He tried to open his eyes, but they were so heavy. "Violet!" he yelled and fought to wake up. His hands felt like they were tied to anchors, why couldn't he lift them? "VIOLET!" He thrashed against the weight.

"Shhhh, buddy. You're gonna mess up the pretty doc's digs here, man and she'll kick us out before she saves your ass."

"Sebastian?" Max stilled, his eyes open to slits. "Where is Vi? Is she safe?"

"I'm here, Max. Blitz and I are right here. I'd never leave you." He felt her cool hands against his feverish skin and then turned into her voice.

"Shhh, Sebastian, found a doctor and she's going to help you, but you have to stay still, babe. The bullet is still in your side, and she needs to get it out as quickly as possible." Her voice cracked.

"Had to tie ya down, man, don't want you kicking your own ass while doc digs the little bastard out," he heard Seb say.

He opened his eyes wider at Violet. He took in her ripped shirt, her nipples poking against the homemade crop top. He grunted at her. "Babe, you need a sweatshirt. Seb is an asshole."

He heard Sebastian laugh and felt his hand come down on his shoulder. "He's gonna live."

When he woke up again, his body felt cooler, but there

was still heat all around him. He squinted into the dark room, getting his bearings. He felt the weight to his right shift into him gently and breathe deeply. He turned to her, nuzzling her hair. Her small hand was lying across his heart and her body was tight to his good side. He turned his head left and found the weight on his left leg was Blitz. He could tell the dog had been careful not to lie against his wound, but, of course, he hadn't been too far from his side.

He tried to open his eyes more fully. His side was a dull throb, but he knew he'd be fine. She'd saved him. He closed his eyes and shuddered out a deep breath.

He'd wanted to die after losing Alex. He had practically willed himself to die alongside him in that shithole safe house alleyway. He hadn't understood why he got to live and Alex didn't at the time, but now he knew. He'd lived to love this woman. She was it for him and he would do anything to protect her. He would figure out this puzzle and he would ensure her safety. She was his life. He turned back to her and fell asleep with his lips pressed into her soft hair.

CHAPTER TWENTY TWO

VIOLET

"Vi, please get a sweatshirt. You're killing me, babe, and I don't think the doctor would be happy with me if I did what I'm dying to do to you." She felt Max's words rumble from his throat. She stretched against him and then glared at him.

"Max, do NOT talk to me about dying right now."

"Too soon?" He grinned up at her.

She dropped down to him and kissed him deeply. She had been so scared of losing him. His right hand came up behind her neck and held her to him, their hearts beating against one another.

"Oh good, lover boy is awake," she heard Sebastian mutter. He'd been asleep in the chair at the end of Max's bed. She tried to sit up, but Max held her to him.

"Babe, I'm not sure what happened to your shirt, but sweet Jesus, you really are killing me. Your nipples are poking me and I can see the underside of your gorgeous tits. I love it, you're sexy as fuck, but I don't want to have to kill Seb after he went to all of this trouble to help us."

She had completely forgotten how she'd ditched her bra and shredded her shirt to make a tourniquet for his wound last night. She felt heat suffuse her cheeks and she leaned back from Max enough to place her arm across her breasts, holding the shirt firm to her skin.

"Her quick thinking saved your ass, buddy. I'd never seen a bra act as a giant-ass Band-Aid, but hey, I've seen bras used for weirder things." Seb laughed.

She sat up fully as the doctor joined them. The doctor was a young woman, probably in her late twenties and absolutely stunning. Violet looked down at herself and then met the doctor's eyes.

"It's OK, Violet, thank goodness you did what you did! Please, grab a shower in my bathroom just down the hall. I ran out and got you some new underwear, a bra, and clothes. There's coffee and some scones on the kitchen counter. I'll just check Max and then you can maybe get him cleaned up more. Lord knows I do NOT want to do that part." The doctor laughed.

"Doc is actually Tad's sister Lauren. This is her place," she heard Seb say. When she looked at him again, Seb said, "Tad was on our team too. He's out of town now, which is why you got me and not him as your escort from the boat last night."

"It's true, Tad is my big brother and I've been around these guys now for years. I promise, this house is safe and you're OK to leave him to get cleaned up and get something to eat and drink. I, myself, am three cups of coffee deep and those scones are buttermilk, oatmeal-cherry. Chef's kiss, Violet, trust me." Lauren smiled at her again.

"A shower sounds almost as amazing as that scone and coffee, Lauren, thank you so much." Violet slid from the bed, trying not to jostle Max and his injury. She'd just cleared the bed when he grabbed her wrist. She looked down into his warm eyes, her smile kicking up at seeing him alive and awake this morning. He pulled her hand to his mouth and kissed her palm before curling her fingers back around the kiss.

Her shower felt divine. She scrubbed her body until it felt raw, but the visual of Max's blood dried onto her hands still made her feel nauseous. She could have lost him last night, right after she'd found him. He'd never hesitated to put himself between her and the bullets flying at her. He'd saved her time and time again and she knew, this man was hers.

Resolute, she shut off the shower, dried herself off, and got dressed. She poured a couple of cups of coffee and carried them back into the room she'd left the others in. Seb jumped up to help her, and between the two of them, they all had coffee and scones while Lauren probed Max's wound and declared, "He'll live."

She hated to darken the mood so quickly, but she was ready to face these assholes. "How did they find us? There's no tie to that house except for Luke. Oh my God, Hazel!" She sat up, frantic for her sister. She couldn't believe it had taken her this long to think about Hazel!

"Shhh, she's good, Vi. I talked to Luke a bit ago and they're fine. Truly. You can call them now if you want," Seb reassured her.

"I'd actually love to call them, yes, please. Not because I don't believe you but because I really need to hear my sister's voice or I may officially lose it."

Lauren laughed. Seb immediately pulled his phone out and dialed Luke.

"He OK?" Luke asked as a greeting.

"Yeah, man, he's still ugly and old, but he'll live," Seb responded.

Everyone laughed at that, even though Max's laugh was rusty and cut off with a little grunt of pain. "I'm three months older than you, fucker," he said to Seb.

"Luke, is Hazel there? I just need to hear her voice," Violet said.

"Yep, hang tight one minute. She has her earbuds in and is currently not talking to me," Luke replied. Violet met Max's eyes, questioning what that was about. He reached for her hand and squeezed it.

"Vi! Oh, thank God. My babysitter, who is an asshole by the way, has been giving me zero details outside of the 'she's fine,' lines. How are you? Are you OK?" Hazel shrieked into the line.

There was a shuffle over the line and some arguing back and forth before Hazel clicked over to speakerphone.

"Warden Luke says I need to be on speaker, so don't tell me about your sex life or anything juicy," Hazel joked. At that comment, Violet felt Max's hand tighten on hers.

"That's OK, sis. I'm on speaker too with Max, Seb, and Lauren. We're in Narragansett, I think. I honestly don't know but I do know Luke is just trying to keep you safe." Violet told Hazel. "We probably shouldn't talk long, but I needed to hear your voice."

"I love you, Vi. I'm good. Warden Luke is thorough so I'm sure I'll still be under house arrest by the time you guys solve this thing," Hazel replied.

Luke spoke again. "We think that they found you when you started searching Ambassador Neil's accounts. Mila has been hacked and has desperately been fighting off cyber assault on all fronts. She is miserable that her bestie has been shot at and that her Maxie has been shot. She has Wills with her now for help and cover. They've been able to block the blitzes from dark hats, but they can see that we're dealing with professionals here that are extremely well funded and extremely smart."

Luke's heavy words landed hard on all of them. This was big.

Max spoke again, "but this means we are on the right path. This is the hunt or we wouldn't have been attacked, physically or online. It has to be the Tunisian routes and it can't be legal product being moved or there wouldn't be such a desire to keep it hidden."

"He's right," Seb said. "This is the hunt. We need to know the players now."

"Boys, it's time to play offense in this ugly game. We need hard evidence and the only way to get that is from the source himself," Max said.

"Are you thinking what I'm thinking Max?" Seb asked.

"Hell yes, Seb. Let's put this fucker down. Call in the others," Max said.

"Ooo-Ah!" Seb pumped his fist in the air and Lauren snorted at him. "DC, here we come."

CHAPTER TWENTY THREE

MAX

It would take a couple of days to put the pieces in place to pull off any type of skirmish with Ambassador Neil. The assholes had proven they were good, but they'd also shown their collective hand. Max and his team knew they had to set the trap, they just needed Neil to take the bait. Whatever was on the video could be the proof they needed, but they needed to regroup before they crossed that bridge. Live to see another day and all of that.

Sebastian left the room to get some coffee and take his own shower and Lauren was off to work. It was important that her schedule didn't change much in case anyone was paying attention, but she had hated to leave them all. He'd watched the lingering looks between her and Seb and, damn, if he didn't know better, Tad was going to kill Seb for touching his sister. Max was kind of excited to see that go down. Lauren was her own person, she could make her own decisions, even though Tad would never see that.

He was propped up now, drinking coffee. Violet had gone to get some warm towels for a little sponge bath, and he was eager to get that party started, although the last thing Lauren had said to both of them before she left was "No nakey tickle time, guys, it is too soon." He'd pouted and laughed at the scarlet flame that shot up Vi's neck.

Vi came in and set the hot washcloths down next to a bowl of steaming water. They'd cut his shirt off last night, so she only had to slide his pants down his legs. Tortuous. His dick didn't get the memo that he wasn't being called into action and Vi had to physically pull the seam of his pants up over him and then down. Her mouth had been *right there*. Fucking cock-blocking motherfuckers. Neil's mercenaries should be killed for the sole fact of keeping him from showing Vi how much he adored her.

She set her hand low on his belly without touching his cock. "Babe, you heard Lauren. I'm going to clean you, feed you, and give you a painkiller. Those are the things your body needs right now." She met his eyes, dark eyes warm and earnest on his.

"My body will always need you, Vi." He couldn't look away from her. She leaned down and kissed him, right on the heart.

"Your body will always have me, Max," she demurred, "just not *that* way this morning." She quickly kissed the side of his mouth and pulled back.

She pumped a little soap into the washcloth and gently ran it down his neck and chest before getting it wet again. Her movements were reverent on his skin, and she worked methodically to keep the cloth hot. Still at attention, his dick got a quick kiss as she washed him last. It was utilitarian until the little kiss on the tip and the wicked look in her eyes.

"Violet," he growled. Her laughter tinkled across him, and he felt his own mouth stretch into a smile, watching her.

"I'll be right back, Max, I'm going to go get fresh water to rinse you." She dropped the cloth into the bowl and left the room. His eyes started to droop closed. His energy was waning. He heard her come back in the room and felt her gentle ministrations on his body. She made quicker work of it this time.

"Max, babe, eat a bite of this scone and then take this painkiller, your body will get better rest." She caressed his jaw. He turned his mouth into her hand and kissed her palm again before opening his eyes.

She helped him sit up a little more and then fed him small bites of the scone. He ate the entire thing and then she helped him get a drink of his coffee. He washed the painkiller down with a little water and then laid back down to close his eyes once again.

He felt her tracing the numbers tattooed across his heart. "Alex's birthday," he whispered, right before he fell asleep again.

His sleep was deep and dreamless this time. When he woke back up, she was asleep in the chair at the foot of the bed and Seb had his feet up on the side of his bed while he reclined in the chair next to him.

"Blitz is passed out on the couch in the living room. Brother, your dog is snoring his head off. He liked the steak Vi made him for lunch," Sebastian said. "I thought you were a goner for her, but you're not as bad as your dog."

He groaned and rolled to face his friend as smoothly as possible. He needed to go to the bathroom and damned if he was going to make Seb hold his hand for that. He willed his legs to slide off and sat on the side of the bed until the nausea passed and the bile left his throat.

"You stubborn fucker." Seb sighed as he came around the side of the bed to help him out of the bed. "I'll get you there and back, but you're holding your own dick. I have standards on where I put my hands." Max dropped his head back and laughed quietly.

"Dude, we both know your standards are total shit. But hey, good news, I have no intention of letting you touch my dick," Max fired back.

Once he was back in bed with a much calmer bladder, he eased himself to a semi-reclined position while Seb held up a glass of water for him and helped him take a drink.

"I'm glad to see this for you, Max." Seb spoke softly to him, so as to not wake Vi. "She's good for you. She's in love with you. God knows why."

"I love her, Seb." Max responded just above a whisper. He knew he loved her and he wanted to tell everyone, but she deserved to hear those words from him directly and not whispered around her while she dozed.

"I know, buddy, I know," Seb replied. "If you're up to it, we have some information to review from Mila and Wills." He picked up a notepad from the desk behind his chair.

"Ambassador Neil has been receiving payments of several million, once a quarter for the last two years in a Swiss bank account. He also was paying out a very small portion of that each quarter to at least three other accounts that we've found so far. One of those, we've tracked to accounts in the Bahamas belonging to Brandon Mills, one son of the Speaker of the House of the good ol' US of A," Seb reported.

"We're trying to figure out the other two accounts and where he's getting whatever he's selling. If we're lucky, one of those other two accounts could answer both of those big questions, but these are deep waters, my friend. They have stuff really well buried."

"Have we run everything on that port of authority board of commissioners?" Max asked.

"They're working their way through the list now and no hits, but they have a few more of those folks to go," Seb replied.

"What about the Speaker of the House?" Violet's quiet voice piped in.

CHAPTER TWENTY FOUR

VIOLET

She had awoken to hear about the money-moving accounts. God, what had Brandon been doing? It struck her at her core to hear he was involved, not because she had known him well or cared deeply for him, but she was convinced he tried to get her out of the mess she'd inadvertently waded into and he'd paid the price for that with his life. It might have been wishful thinking on her part, but she had to assume the good in people.

"We have to act as if Speaker Mills is part of this. We can't will him to be innocent and be stabbed in the back by the biggest player on the board," Max replied. Seb was shaking his head in agreement when they heard the front door open. Seb and Max both had guns in their hands before they heard Lauren ring out, "Just me, put your guns away, I have pasta!"

"Where in the hell were you keeping that gun, Max?!" Vi exclaimed at the same time Seb asked, "How did she know that we had our guns out from in there?"

Lauren came to the door. "These boys and their guns, am I right?" Vi laughed with her.

"Come into the kitchen and eat guys, I picked up the best pasta and breadsticks in town. Max, I know you want to get up and sit with us and I know your stubborn ass is OK to do so, so come on. Out of bed you go, lazy bones," Lauren said.

The pasta was actually divine, God bless Lauren for more than just saving Max's life. Although that fact alone had made her a Lauren devotee for life. She glanced over at Max as he laughed lightly with Seb and her heart turned over. She loved this man.

He caught her eyes and reached over, gathering her hand and pulling her close. She nuzzled into his good side. He dropped a kiss to the top of her head as he kept talking to Seb. This was the kind of life she had hoped for. The love of this amazing man, friends laughing at a dinner table together. It made her remember the lively dinner table conversations that she grew up with. Her parents were always making her and Hazel join in the conversation, whether about politics or art or history. The world needed more dinner tables!

She sat up. Her mind was racing, her spine stiff. Max stopped talking and looked at her as did Seb and Lauren.

"Babe, are you OK?" Max asked her, tense now that she was too. She stood up and paced through the kitchen, pausing to look back at the three expectant faces tracking her every move.

"The table. We were at a fundraising dinner when this all started. A fundraising dinner with assigned seating down a long, communal table overlooking the battlefield. When I found Brandon after a bit, he'd been sitting back down at the table in our spots. That's when I found him with Neil and spilled about the video. What if we hack into the event planner's files and look for a seating chart? Maybe see other people who could be players in this." She rushed the words out, the rightness of it feeling weighty in her gut.

"Hot damn, woman! Max, she's too smart for you." Seb clapped.

"It might not be the lead we're looking for, but it could be the break we need," Vi added.

Lauren jumped up and hugged her. "Yes, Vi, great thinking!" She hugged her again.

Violet walked back over to Max and put her hand on his shoulder, "Max, this feels right."

Max pulled her back down onto his lap as softly as possible with his good arm. "I agree, Vi, let's connect in the others and see what we can find."

Sebastian cleared the dishes while Lauren went to take a shower, letting Blitz back in from the backyard when she passed the door. He came in and went straight to Violet, nudging her hand for more treats. She slipped him a breadstick before Seb grabbed her plate. "I saw that," Max growled in her ear.

She squirmed on his lap. "And I feel that, sweetheart. Please stop before I lose the blood to my brain for my cock," he grumbled into her ear.

"Knock it off, you two, we have work to do," Seb interrupted. He was right, they had a good lead and they needed to dig in.

"As long as Max agrees to move over to the couch and then rest when his body tells him to. He was shot like twenty-four hours ago," she demanded and sat up, reaching back to help him stand.

"I'll be a good boy, for now." He added the last two words under his breath for her ears alone.

Seb loaded the dishwasher and joined them in the living room, which opened to the dining room table. It wasn't a large home, but it felt so cozy and safe with all of them there. She sent up a prayer of gratitude for these people who were keeping her safe and trying to help her.

Seb placed his phone on the coffee table between his chair and the couch they were sitting on, dialing Luke. "Yo," Luke answered.

"We have a lead," Max said in the direction of the phone.

"About time, my guys. Let me connect in Mila and Wills. I have Brian, Theo, and Nate securing and preparing our home base in Dupont Circle for when we get over there. We were almost ready with it and they're cranking out those finishing pieces now. We'll fill them in when we get there," Luke said.

"Where is Tad again?" Max asked.

"Yeah, where is Tad again?" Lauren added, walking into the room, rubbing her wet hair with a towel. She had on small sleep shorts and a little white tank top, dampened down the front from her long hair, something Seb's eyes seemed unable to look away from. He cleared his throat.

"You wouldn't believe me if I told you. And also, I'm not telling you fuckers. He told me not to, but he should be back tomorrow night," Seb answered.

"Mmmmkay, that doesn't sound like some stupid booty call or anything," Lauren retorted.

"Children, focus!" Luke laughed.

Max's wound was starting to pull again and itch at the sides. He'd allow himself one more pain pill and then no more of the strong stuff. He'd switch to Tylenol and ibuprofen. He wanted to stay alert, but he knew his body needed the rest too.

He swept his hand along Vi's thigh, ending at her knee and squeezing gently. "Violet has a brilliant idea," he said.

"Hells ya she did!" Hazel exclaimed from the speaker. Violet smiled, she missed her sister.

"Hey, sis!" she called toward the phone on the table.

"She's back to talking to me, guys, and honestly, now she won't stop talking," Luke said.

"Shut it, Warden Luke-a-licious," Hazel retorted. Oh Lord, Vi could practically hear her sister sticking out her tongue at Luke. They heard a deep, tortured sigh from Luke.

"I take it Hazel has met Mila." Vi laughed.

"Yes, joy ensued. Clearly." Luke deadpanned.

Violet had snuggled into Max's good side again when they sat down and now she turned into his side to face him and Seb. She placed both hands on his leg and squeezed, physically connected to him as closely as possible for the moment.

Lauren took the other chair across from them while Luke connected the calls.

"Bestie! Maxie! Are you guys OK? I am SO sorry. I got

cocky," her voice trailed off and they heard a deep murmur in the background. "I'm really sorry. It's my fault. I was paying too much attention to the wormholes I had set and fell into one of theirs." She spoke softly now, her typical sunshine missing.

"We've got it now though. We're Fort Knox over here and Mila has you all covered better than anyone I've ever worked with." A new voice had joined the call.

"Hey, Willsy," Seb said.

"Seb, Max, Lauren, good to chat. Miss you fuckers. Violet, we haven't met yet but let me know if Max doesn't take care of you. From what I can tell, you're out of his league. And, I love the guy, so I'm giving him extra points for my love," Wills said. "Oh, and Hazel, nice work busting Luke's balls, keep up the good work."

Everyone laughed. These people felt like her family already. They were showing up for her, based on Luke's call. Well, Luke's call in the beginning, and Max's devotion since then. She looked up at his face again. The lines around his mouth were starting to deepen with pain, and she could see his eyes clouding over. It was time to get this show on the road so he could rest.

"Nice to meet you, Wills, thank you for helping me get out of this mess. Truly, thank you all." She paused, getting a little knot in her throat. Her voice quivered, it felt like she was talking around a shelf lodged in her throat. "I'd be dead without you all and I can't thank you enough." She finished saying what needed said without crying, which was an early Christmas miracle. She heard a little sniffling over the line.

"Vi, we're your people now. No thanks needed but if you still feel that way once we are all clear of this, make an honest man of our buddy. He needs you," Wills said.

Max leaned forward and kissed her lips so quickly, her blush was still blazing across her face when he leaned back into the couch and closed his eyes.

"Um, thanks, Wills," she replied. She took a deep breath and spoke toward the phone.

"OK, guys, we had assigned seating at the party that night and when I found Brandon again, right before we left, he had sat back down in our assigned seats at the table. That's where I found him and Ambassador Neil. I'm wondering if maybe my video caught someone talking to them before I got over there. Ambassador Neil had been close during dinner but not immediately next to either Brandon or me. Do you think we could hack the event planner's files and get our hands on the seating chart?" Vi asked.

Wills spoke up, "Mila was working on it before you finished talking Violet, great thinking."

"I'll need to sift through this tonight. I need to slow down and be thorough. I'm so sorry again, guys. I think it's best if I go slower and circle the dark web to cover my tracks better so I don't leave anyone exposed again. I won't let you down again," Mila said. There were more murmured low words from the line. It was clear to all of them that Wills was comforting Mila. She was really beating herself up.

"Mila, Bestie, it's OK." Violet smiled, her warmth seeping into her voice. "You've helped far more than you've hurt and we're going to be fine."

"Thanks, Vi, give Maxie a kiss for me," Mila responded.

They disconnected after that with agreement to talk again tomorrow. Seb took Blitz out and checked the perimeter while Lauren and Vi helped Max back to the bed in the guest bedroom. They sat him on the edge while Lauren checked his wound and Vi grabbed him a glass of water and a pain pill.

"You're too tough to be down for long, Max, this looks so much better already," Lauren said.

"It itches like a motherfucker," he groused.

Lauren laughed. "No pouty patients allowed here, Max." She patted his shoulder and murmured a quiet "good night," to them before stepping out of the room.

She left the door open and Seb followed Blitz in. "All good here, brother." He helped Max stand and make his way to the bathroom. He waited for Max to come back out and then helped him back over to the bed. Blitz was snuggled into where Max had been lying earlier and jumped down when they got close.

"Get your beauty sleep, ya ugly mug," Seb said and picked up Max's legs and swung them into the bed, surprisingly gently. He winked at Vi and was out the door, closing it softly behind him.

The glow from the lamp beside the bed illuminated Violet's creamy skin, and she shed the leggings and sweatshirt she'd worn all day. She removed her bra and was now bared before him. Her creamy curves on gorgeous display. He groaned low in his throat and patted the bed next to him. "I know I can't have you but I need to feel those curves against me."

"Hang on, let me find a T-shirt," she replied.

"No, I need to feel you bare." She knew he was talking about her skin and yet she felt wetness gather at her core, thinking about him sinking into her bare, most intimate skin to most intimate skin.

My God, her head was in the gutter. This man had taken a bullet for her one day ago and she was thinking about sex with him. She shook her head slightly to free those rampant thoughts and slipped between the cool sheets. She laid her head on his chest, the pads of her fingers tracing his tattoos again. She wanted to know the story of each and every one of them. She wanted hours and days, months and years of tracing these stories across his chest and hearing his voice rumble through her. He kissed her head and settled in.

She waited until his breathing had evened out, kissing the space on his chest that protected his beautiful heart. "I love you, Max."

CHAPTER TWENTY FIVE

MAX

The smell of frying bacon woke him up and he opened his eyes slowly. His dreams had been of his dark-haired girl and she was snuggled against his side, bare breasts tucked against his chest and her small hand low on his belly. He felt a little wet spot on his chest from her drool and grinned up at the ceiling. This girl.

He kissed the top of her head. "Vi. Baby. Smells like Seb is making breakfast." He kissed her head again and the arm wrapped around her slid down to her butt. He gathered a cheek and rubbed, his fingers firm before he opened his palm to give equal opportunity to her other cheek. He caressed and grabbed, murmuring her name against her head as she slowly opened her eyes. They were hazy with lust and she grinned at him and slid over on top of him, gently placing her knee wide outside of his injured side.

"Mmmmmm," he heard her straight-up purr as she kissed down his neck.

His dick took notice. "Yes please," he thought. This sleepy woman working her way down his body, warm skin to warm skin was the perfect way to wake up.

"Max, she breathed, lay very still so you don't injure your-self further." She looked back up at him from where her mouth had sucked a little path to the sharp V of muscles leading to his cock. Her smile was pure sin as she cradled him in her small hand and licked a path up around the tip.

Maybe he had died. This certainly felt like heaven. His hands gathered her hair away from her face so he could see his dick disappearing down her throat. She licked and laved, sucked and pulled. Her lips were glistening around his hardness and he knew he wouldn't last much longer. He saw her reach her hand down to herself and felt her moan on his dick.

"Christ, Vi, I'm going to come down your throat." He tightened his grip on her hair.

Her only response was to shudder against him as her hand worked her clit. He could really die a happy man right now, watching her get herself off with his dick in her mouth. He felt her start to tremble and he knew she was as close as he was.

"Viiiiiii, baby." His guttural cry came out hoarse and quiet as he unloaded down her throat. He felt her mouth contract more tightly around him, practically milking him as her body convulsed against his. Her hand came away from herself wet as she wrapped it around the base of his cock. She gently sucked once more and then licked her way back up his body, fixating on the grooves of his abs.

He held her hair in one hand and pushed her head to his, kissing her thoroughly.

"Good morning, baby." She smiled against his mouth. He chuckled darkly against her. "Good morning."

That morning, he was able to get out of bed and get to the bathroom on his own. Once he'd done what he needed to and brushed his teeth, he stepped out into the guest room for Vi to get a hot shower.

She brushed her nakedness against him in the small space of the doorway and he leaned down to suck on her neck while his thumb snuck up and rolled her nipple between his thumb and fingers.

"Careful, or we won't make it to breakfast and Lauren will be mad I broke open my stitches pinning you to this door and fucking you senseless." His growled promise echoed in the small space.

Her eyes glazed over. "Right. We're saving that for later for sure." She gulped and stepped further into the bathroom for her shower.

"That's a promise, Vi," he said and winked at her.

In the main area of the house, he could see Seb at the stove finishing up breakfast for them. He had poured him a cup of coffee as he walked across the living room and set it on the counter as Max pulled up a stool.

"Well, well, well, don't you look smug and freshly fuck-faced," Seb intoned.

Max did not feel one bit bad about looking smug and fuck-faced. He felt smug and he supposed fuckfaced was a pretty good look too. He had the most amazing woman by his side and he knew his team was smarter than whoever was after them. He knew they'd take care of business and his heart felt lighter than it had in ages.

He'd also spied the couch, which hadn't been slept on, so he needled Seb right back.

"Have you looked in the mirror, asshole? Don't think that I've missed the situation between you and Lauren. Tad is going to murder you if you hurt her." He leveled a gaze at his buddy. "Shit, man, we will take turns killing you if you hurt her."

Seb snorted at him, "More like if she hurts me, man." His eyes flashed and Max decided to drop it, for now.

Lauren had left for work with strict instructions to call her if his wound felt hot. She knew he was smart enough to call her if something felt off. They'd all been around gunshot wounds long enough to know the drill.

Seb plated up some bacon, fruit, and homemade, cinna-mon-sugar muffins for all of them as Vi came into the kitchen.

"Oh my gosh, do you all cook?" Vi exclaimed, making the "gimmie" motion with her hands as Seb held out a cup of coffee for her.

"Yes, kind of. Some of us are better than others, namely me. I'm the best," Seb said.

"Don't let him fool you, sweetheart." Max wrapped his arm around her waist as she leaned against him. "He only made the muffins because he knows Lauren loves them." Seb smacked his hand with the spatula.

"Enough." Seb's mouth had hardened slightly. "I'll spoil her whenever she lets me."

Max and Violet exchanged a look. He knew she'd want all of the details later. He didn't have many, but it didn't take a genius to see Lauren and Seb were something. Something enough that Tad would be popping up soon with some questions.

Violet eased onto the stool next to him and the three of them ate their breakfast, chatting about possible products the ambassador could be moving.

"I still think it's weapons. The proximity is just too real to ignore," Max said. "The correct answer is most often the simplest answer."

"I agree, and frankly, the alternative is humans or drugs. Drugs don't make sense for those routes and humans are less likely into Tunisia," Seb added.

"Humans?" Vi asked, "is that a real concern for today for women out of DC and NYC?"

The men looked at each other. "Unfortunately, yes. There are some real-deal assholes out there, Vi." Seb said.

She shivered and scooted her stool closer to Max's. They finished up breakfast together and then Vi offered to clean up the kitchen while Max carefully made his way to the shower and Seb took Blitz outside to play.

They spent the day talking through scenarios about each of the party guests that Violet could remember seeing and could name. She'd made a list of them when they were at the cottage around Little Compton, but it had been left on the desk there when they'd fled. They re-created that and, between the three of them, added as many details about each person as they could. They worked steadily throughout the day with

Max dozing off and on in the afternoon while Sebastian and Violet kept the notes flowing.

When Lauren got home later that night, the sun had long since set and it was cold. Late fall on the coast of New England had set in and Seb had started the fireplace in the cozy living area to take the nip out of the air.

Lauren took a quick shower and then joined them in the living area as Violet made dinner in the open kitchen.

"Vi, that smells incredible, you might need to move in with me!" Lauren sat down next to Max on the couch and he glared at her.

"No" was his entire response to that. Lauren laughed at him.

Vi could live wherever she wanted, he'd follow her any-where, but she'd be living with him, thank you very much.

"I hope you guys like this, it's actually something I make often, kind of my comfort meal." She stirred the bubbling orzo.

"I'm just glad I had the ingredients in my pantry and refrigerator. If you all had fled a hail of bullets twenty-four hours earlier than you did, we'd be out of luck. I had just gro-cery shopped the day you all showed up," Lauren replied. "I had just been planning on Seb . . ." she trailed off awkwardly, meeting Max's eyes with a flash of fear.

"I'm gonna leave that right there because you saved my life," he whispered to her.

Seb and Violet ignored the comment too. Violet plated the gooey orzo for them and brought the shallow dishes to each of them with forks. "Living room picnic!" She laughed.

"Eating on my couch is my norm, so this feels perfect. Thanks, Vi." Lauren smiled up at Vi.

Once they were all settled and eating, they filled Lauren in on their work from the day. They were almost halfway through the list with her when she dropped her fork into her dish. It clattered over the edge onto the floor.

"Wait, back up one name," she said.

"Brady Scott," Vi read again from her notes, "big family, NYC based, that's all we really know about him. I only knew who he was because he checked in right in front of Brandon and me."

"I went to school with Brady at Harvard. He's an asshole of the highest order," Lauren said. "His family is big, you have that right. He has three brothers and they are all in the city, living outrageously."

"Where does the money come from?" Max asked.

"I don't know where it comes from originally, I think their mom maybe. But honestly, those boys go through more money than you and I can even dream of, and my parents do pretty well as you know," Lauren responded.

"So, we have four brothers, all living in the city, living lavish lifestyles of the rich and famous, one of them was there that night and checked in *right in front* of Brandon," Seb mused.

Violet nodded her head.

"Did they talk, Vi? Did they sit close to you?" Max asked.

"They didn't talk at all when we checked in, but Brady and his date did sit close to us, maybe three people away? Brady was on the other side, facing toward us. It was one of the long, communal-style tables set up across that huge expanse of overlook by the cannons," she replied. "Looking back, they hardly even looked at each other at dinner. Brady's date was that supermodel, Ilyana something or other and she kept trying to make small talk, but Brandon seemed ensconced in the conversation next to him instead. I actually felt bad for her because she was kind of stuck between guys who really didn't talk much to her, but she was across and down one from me, so I couldn't talk to her without yelling awkwardly."

"Isn't it almost weird that they didn't talk much? I mean, they were right next to each other checking in and no pleasantries? They have to know each other. NYC is actually pretty small in those circles and then they hardly talked at dinner even though they were practically right across from each other?" Max pursed his lips.

"I don't like this, you guys. The simplest answer is most often the correct one."

Seb's phone rang with Luke's name flashing across the screen.

"Luke, what's up man? We think we may have just discovered something." Seb answered on speaker, so they could all talk.

"Hazel's apartment has been hit." Luke gave it to them bluntly. "She's fine, obviously she wasn't there and is with me, but they tossed the place pretty good, and she is shaken up. These assholes are good too, guys. They knew to evade the cameras I had and the standard ones in Hazel's area. Mila has already hacked the traffic cam feeds and the security feeds from Hazel's building. I had two in her apartment, one in the living room and one in her bedroom," Luke went on, and they heard him mumble to Hazel in the background, "I only added them after I met up with you, I'm not a perv."

Luke spoke back into the phone. "They tossed it, made it look like a burglary, and didn't take a single thing. In fact, they left something and you aren't going to like it." They heard him take a deep breath and then his voice hardened.

"They left a bouquet of violets on the counter," he said.

CHAPTER TWENTY SIX

VIOLET

"What?! Why would they do that? What does that mean?" she cried, fear creeping up her spine.

"They want to scare you, babe, it's a mind fuck. You're OK, I've got you, and I am not letting one single fucker get to you," Max promised her. He shifted up on the couch, grimacing slightly as he physically placed himself between her and the phone. "Not one single motherfucker is getting close to her." He slammed his fist on the coffee table, rattling the phone.

"Max, man, we know. We've got you both. Chill." Seb held his arm out, his hand down as if to hold Max back.

"They're trying to scare you, Vi," Luke said. "It is exactly a mind fuck, like Max said." He went on, "They were smart to avoid the cameras in there but they don't really know where Hazel is. Mila made it look like she's on some eat, pray, chocolate bullshit somewhere in the EU. They left the violets in case you were there or went there to hide out. They're trying to draw you out, Vi."

"It's working. I'm scared. I want to run out there and fight but I don't know where to!" She cried. "My parents! Luke, my parents! Will they go there next?"

"I hope so. I have Brody covering them and he is one crazy fucker. I'd love for him to take some of this crew off the playing board. But I don't think they'll go there. Mila also made it seem like they'd moved down to Boca to some ritzy medically assisted living center for memory care. That place has great security, so they won't mess with it just to scare you. No, I think they'll keep after Hazel and that isn't happening for them," he replied.

Max looked back at Vi, his eyes promising her safety. She snuggled back into him as he sat back slightly, still physically in front of her shoulder. He was not taking this well.

"We're close to something though, guys. Tell them what we discovered," Lauren said.

"Hang on, I know Mila and Wills were in the files from the event-planning company, let's conference them in," Luke went on.

He connected them in again and Violet outlined what they discussed. They could hear the clacking of keyboard keys as they talked. Mila interrupted, "That's it!"

"I dug into Brady Scott and his brother, Philip, is on the board at the New York and New Jersey Port Authority. He's on that board of commission, you guys, this has to be it!"

"So, we have Brandon, potentially Speaker Mills, Brady Scott, and Philip Scott. Are there any other players we know of, outside of the army of assholes doing their wet work?" Max asked.

"No, that's all we have. But we still don't know what the product is," Seb said.

"Brandon's mom's family is Pell Weaponry though, he has unfettered access, it has to be weapons," Max reminded everyone.

"I agree with Max. And, we keep following the money," Luke replied. "It's always about the money."

"Um, guys, I think I know how to get more information," Mila cut in. "There's another fundraiser coming up in two days, and it's at Ambassador Neil's townhome on Embassy Row."

Max and Seb looked at each other. "Sounds like it is time

to get to DC." Max said.

They made plans to fly out the next morning. Luke would have a private plane waiting for them at Westerly to take them to a smaller airstrip right outside of the metro of DC. From there, they'd converge on the safe house the rest of their team had set up.

Violet softly closed the door to their room, her eyes meeting Max's as he sat back in the bed. They could both hear the terse arguing happening in the primary room next to theirs. Sebastian felt very strongly that Lauren should be going with them, and Lauren felt very strongly that she needed to stay there for her patients. They had no reason to believe that anyone could tie her to anything happening and she was not budging.

"I've never heard Seb so domineering with a woman before," Max mused.

"Maybe he has never cared as much before. Have you seen how he looks at her, Max?"

"No. I only see you, babe. Get over here."

Violet flipped the light off and made her way to bed. She stripped down and joined him under the covers. Sliding against him, she felt complete. Like there had always been a big piece missing, she just hadn't known it until he notched against her.

His hands reached for her, grabbing on to her ass and sliding her over him.

"Max! You're going to open your stitches!" she protested, even as she rocked her hips down into his ever so slightly. Her body had a mind of its own apparently, and it wanted him. Desperately.

"Not if you ride me real nice and slow, sweetheart," he murmured against her lips. She felt his callused hands sweeping across her back and then back down to grip her ass in two firm handfuls. He shifted her against his cock, her wetness seeping out, coating him while he slid her hips back and forth against him.

"I'm not even inside of you yet, baby, and you're soaking me," he groaned. She dropped her knees firmly into the mattress at his sides, being careful not to jostle his injury, and rocked her hips back to sink onto him. She teased him a little.

"Slow and easy, baby? Just the tip?" She giggled into his ear as her hands worked their way through his hair. She could see his eyes shining in the darkened room.

"Vi, have mercy on an injured man. Please," he begged, gripping her cheeks harder against himself.

She leaned down and met her mouth to his, sweeping her tongue inside. Kissing him was making her wetter and wetter with his cock sliding against her entrance. She shifted up slightly and nudged her knee out to sink completely onto him. His kiss became ferocious as he ate at her mouth. She ground against him, the pressure right on her clit.

"Max, baby," she keened as she sat up and arched back.

"That's the view I love to see." He smiled up at her and swept his hands around to her breasts. He worked them both, squeezing and pinching, rolling her nipples, sweeping those huge, rough hands across her collarbone and down to her belly.

She sat up further and put her hands on his chest, angling down on him while she picked up speed on his cock. It was torture, exquisite and throbbing torture. He pulsed inside of her, hot and hard, making her gasp. His hand snaked around and grabbed her hair, tugging it firmly.

She started to shake on top of him, coming apart on him, her gorgeous breasts bouncing in his face. Her wetness coated him and he pulsed inside her, coming apart as she contracted in orgasm around him. She slowed, riding out their joint aftershocks. Locked on him, gazing down at him, she reached up her hand, and cupped his jaw.

"I love you, Max. I know we're new and haven't defined what this is, but I love you. I think I've been waiting for you." She breathed out quietly, her eyes never leaving his.

His smile widened across his face and his hands gathered

her head and drew her back down, flush against his heated body. She propped her elbows across his chest, looking at him with tenderness. He ran his fingers through her hair, watching her.

"Violet, I think I've loved you since you came out of the bathroom in a sweatshirt and jeans that first night. You never fell apart, you're a warrior. You saved my life with your heart before you ever saved my life on the cliffs that night. I've been waiting for you too, and I'm never letting you go. I love you so much."

Her eyes welled up with tears. This wonderful man, this Marine who was willing to die for her, was the other half of her heart. They kissed again for what could have been minutes or hours, she didn't know. She fell asleep kissing him and nuzzling him.

They left early the next morning before the sun was even hinting at the horizon over the ocean. Vi was sad to leave this little enclave of safety and love. The time here had changed everything for her, shifting her life into place.

CHAPTER TWENTY SEVEN

MAX

Lauren won the battle with Sebastian to stay in her normal routine and live her life in Narragansett as if nothing was happening, and the fucker was super cranky about it. Seb walked toward the chartered plane with Blitz at his side, muttering about strong-willed women who thought they knew everything. Blitz must have heard an earful already with the way he looked at Max and Violet.

They boarded the Bombardier Challenger 3500 in Westerly, bound for DC. The inside of the jet was nicer than most hotels Violet had seen, and standing inside waiting on them, she received the best surprise.

"Hazel!" she cried, launching herself at her sister.

Hazel had been waiting inside of the jet as they made their way up the stairs and stepped back to let them all on. She was hugging Vi fiercely and kissing her face like a happy puppy.

"Vi! Oh my God! I am so happy to see you and feel you." She got teary-eyed and sniffled through the smile on her face. "And, Max! We haven't met, but thank you. You saved my sister! Oh my God, thank you!" She dropped one arm from Vi and reached for him, encircling him in a one-handed hug and bringing him into their embrace.

"She actually saved me. Twice physically," he gruffly responded.

Hazel watched as her sister smiled up at Max, her heart in her eyes. "We're together, Hazey, Max is my . . . everything."

He leaned down and captured her lips with his as Hazel

backed up a step and clapped her hands together. "Swoon! Yes, I love this for us!" She laughed.

Sebastian stepped in after them. "Ya, it's always fucking flowers and heart eyes with these two, you've been warned. Right, Blitz?" Seb looked down at the dog. Blitz just wagged his tail, he was smart to stay out of it really.

Max walked toward the seats, pulling Vi along with him. "I take it Luke-a-licious is flying us today?" he asked.

"That's right, assholes," they heard from the cockpit. "Hey, Vi, love ya, sit down. I want to get this bird back in the air as quickly as possible. Tad is covering our tail number to land in a very tight window outside of the metro," Luke yelled.

They all took their seats while Luke finished his precheck. Violet looked back at him and then over at Sebastian. "I hate to be crass, but how are we affording all of this? The plane, the properties, the tech . . ." She looked adorably confused.

"Ohhhh, lover boy still has some secrets, does he?" Seb teased.

Max laughed and reached across Violet, pulling on her buckle as he did so to ensure it was tight for takeoff. He knew she was about to lose her mind.

"Well," he started, "did you know that Luke is actually fairly smart? Who knew, right? I mean, we were all pretty surprised really."

"I heard that, asshole. Big words when I'm in charge of the altitude and am happy to offer you an adjustment," Luke yelled from the cockpit. Seb cracked up and looked from Vi to Hazel.

"What Max is trying to say is that we're all decently wealthy, actually. Luke has always had a knack for numbers and investments. Our first tour together, we decided to pool most of our earnings together and see what he could do. At the time, we were on let's say 'hazard pay,' and it seemed like a good idea to invest it. Luke had a small trust from his mom that we added to. None of us knew what we were facing back then, but each op we'd add more to the pot. Luke is way smarter than he looks," Seb explained.

"How wealthy are we talking about?" Hazel asked.

"Hazel, that's rude!" Vi admonished.

"Vi, we're talking about Luke, we know everything about it him. Or I thought we did anyway. Our guy is comfortable, and we didn't know about it or he is 'I can rent a private plane' rich and we didn't know about it. There are levels and I want to know which level of subterfuge my warden has been displaying," Hazel said.

Seb and Max exchanged looks, Max shifting uncomfortably. "Actually, he is 'I own this plane and three more like it' rich." Max finally revealed. "And um, I own one too."

"Personally, ladies, I don't own any aircrafts," Seb intoned, very piously.

"No, just a yacht the size of Rhode Island, no big deal." Max rolled his eyes. "And um, actually, Luke owns one of those too." He glanced sheepishly back up to Hazel and Vi.

Just then, Luke came over the speakers, "It's time to ride, guys, we're going up fast, prepare."

The thing about a private jet that you don't know until you are on a private jet is that they can get to altitude very quickly and very steeply. Violet was used to commercial aircraft, which Max told her was more like riding a bus. This jet was more like a jag, and Luke knew how to handle it very, very well.

They were above the clouds, streaks of pale, warm yellows, reds, and oranges shining throughout the cabin before Vi had even processed the level of wealth they'd been talking about.

Luke joined them after setting the autopilot. He stopped at a little bar area and brought them each cups before going back for a carafe of coffee, which he used to fill everyone's cups before he locked it back into place.

"Welcome to my home in the sky, ladies. Sorry I didn't tell you. Honestly, it was really exciting at first and I wanted to shout it from the rooftops, but then I was worried I'd lose it all. I know now that it's safe, in fact, much of the money now is paid out in properties, offshore accounts, suitcases stuffed with cash, you get the idea." He raised apologetic eyes and laughed nervously at Hazel.

For some reason, Hazel was pretty quiet and didn't offer a response.

"Wow, OK," Vi said. "I'm happy for you, Luke, and you, Max, and Seb. That's incredible, truly. I had no idea. Wow."

He could tell she was processing it still and that was unsurprising. Sometimes, he had trouble reconciling it himself. He still wore jeans and T-shirts and drove a Chevy. He had other cars though in a few garages here and there, attached to a few houses he owned. His mom was in one and the other, the other he couldn't imagine actually living in as he and Alex had owned it together. Alex had been part of the investment pool also and they'd dreamed of a shared family vacation house where they'd someday take their wives and kids, watch them play in the waves along the stretch of private beach with their grandma.

With Alex's death so fresh in his heart, he hadn't considered the property or thought about what to do with it. He'd dealt with his brother's estate right after returning stateside, but he'd been in a brain fog then and couldn't process. He had been Alex's beneficiary on everything, which he had immediately locked into trusts for his mom.

"It doesn't change who I am, Vi." He looked over at her pensive face. Shit, was she mad?

"I know, babe." She squeezed his knee affectionately and looked down. "I guess I'm just shocked. I don't really make much and I just quit my role at *Constitution Now*. I'm not really in a position to be an equal contributor to you."

He knew it was safe or Luke wouldn't be on autopilot and sitting with them drinking coffee, so he leaned over her, unbuckled her seat belt, pulled her to him.

She was straddling him now, her face to his. "You aren't equal in this relationship, Vi, you are everything. What's mine is yours, and if you want, we can give it all away," he said, his hands framing her face, eyes focused on her.

"Well, maybe not all, we've all kind of discovered that it's actually harder to get rid of at this level." He laughed but kept his eyes steady on her so she saw his sincerity.

"Really?" she asked. "You'd give it up for me?"

"Vi, baby, I'd do anything for you," he answered, bringing his lips to hers.

"I warned you, Hazel, this is a fairly common thing with these two. It is adorable and sickening, both really," Seb said drolly.

"My ovaries did kind of explode there, guys, maybe wrap that up so the rest of us don't feel like we're about to watch a real-life porno in here," Hazel said.

Max laughed and stopped kissing Vi, but he sure as shit wasn't letting her get off his lap yet. His dick had liked the idea of the mile-high club and needed some time to chill. He eased her back onto his thighs. Too close and he'd lose all blood flow.

They reviewed the plan for landing and getting into DC to the property the other guys had prepared.

"Brian is waiting on us there with an SUV. It's armored, just in case, obviously," Luke said. "Once we get in, we can decide who goes to the event, what type of evidence we need to get, you know the drill."

"Time for me to work again, I guess. We need to hit the window that Tad opened." Luke turned back to the cockpit to begin the descent into the little airport in Northern Virginia.

CHAPTER TWENTY EIGHT

VIOLET

Flying private certainly had its advantages. That was the nicest flight she'd ever been on and the quickest both getting to altitude and getting back down. Hazel had been pretty quiet though and Vi was worried about her. She took her aside when they were disembarking, shooing Max ahead of her to descend the stairs.

"Are you OK, Hazey? What's wrong? Other than the murderous web we're trapped in, I guess," she whispered to her sister.

"Do you feel like we never really knew Luke at all, Vi? He has this whole other life that we knew nothing about. I guess I'm just feeling rocked by it all," Hazel whispered haltingly back to her.

"I hadn't really considered that honestly. Luke is like a big brother out living his own life and I know he has my back whenever I need him, but I guess I hadn't thought about him as a man necessarily," she said as she met Hazel's eyes.

"Vi?" Hazel whispered, even lower. "I've considered him all man for far too long." Tears fell down her face. "And now I realize that I'm not even important enough to be on his radar as a woman. A woman is someone who knows him and whom he knows. I'm just a bratty little sister." She sobbed into Violet's arms.

"Whoa, sis. It's OK. Shhhh." Violet hugged her tightly, not really knowing what to say.

"What the hell, ladies? What's going on here?" Luke came from the cockpit and took one look at them, his eyes snagging on Hazel's face. "Hazelnut, what happened?" he asked.

Violet looked over her sister's head to Luke. "It's OK, Luke, she's just relieved we're both OK. We'll be out in a minute, you go."

He waited a few beats longer. "Are you sure? Hazelnut, you good?"

Hazel stepped back and rubbed at her swollen eyes. "Yeah. Relax Warden Luke-a-licious." Hazel added some snark to her watery voice, hiding the hurt that Vi knew she was feeling.

Luke didn't look convinced, he walked over to the door leading down the stairs and waited for them. "Rejoice in the safety of our home base, please. Our time here has to be fast."

Violet nodded her head and then squeezed Hazel tightly to her chest. "We'll finish this later."

Hazel squeezed back, "No thank you," and disengaged from her.

They descended from the plane to find Max and Luke at the bottom of the stairs, both looking slightly perplexed.

Seb had opened the door to a waiting black Yukon Denali, loading Blitz in first. "Ladies, your chariot awaits." He shooed them in.

Thankfully, the drive to the townhome in Dupont Circle was uneventful. The large, Georgian property had underground parking, and it looked like they were driving right up to it until a door hidden mostly by clever landscaping opened and they pulled inside quickly. It shut behind them immediately and Brian, who had been driving, waited a beat to ensure it was safe before he jumped out and then held the door for Violet and Hazel to climb out of the back seat.

He held out a hand and helped each woman down before closing the SUV and walking in front of them to the door and letting them into the home.

Violet had been renting a flat in DC that was the size of

a postage stamp and had walked by these townhomes a million times, always wondering what the inside might be like. The inside was better than her imagination could ever have dreamed. Notably, this property wasn't one townhome but three conjoined on the inside and made to look like separate units on the outside. She took in the walnut paneling and smoothed her hand along the smooth, dark wainscoting on the wall.

"This place is stunning." She was in awe of the space. Sconces glowed brightly from the walls, and she spied a library on the main floor she walked past with a fire blazing in a hearth that easily took up half the wall. The windows on this floor were mullioned but looked thicker than she'd ever seen before.

"They're bulletproof," Max said, coming up behind her.

"Who owns this place? How in the world did you find it?" she asked.

Max cleared his throat. "Actually, we all kind of own it. We bought it to be a headquarters of sorts, but we weren't sure what type of headquarters. At the time we bought it, all of us were alive and making so much money with Luke's investment portfolios, we just wanted to have a home base here big enough for all of us. Being guys, being Marines, we've added the security layers over the years. We've hired different contractors for different pieces, we've done lots ourselves, we've masked parts of the insides so those hired only saw bits and pieces, you know, kind of just some boys with access and some paranoia," he explained, sheepishly.

"C'mon, I'll show you my space." He tugged her hand and climbed the stairs. He was slower than she knew he normally was and she frowned at his back.

"Max, you need to take it easy. I don't want you reopening your wound or getting an infection," she told him.

"Oh, believe me, baby, you're going to get to play doctor later tonight. And not the kind that is in any way appropriate." He winked back at her and she laughed.

He showed her his "space" as he called it, which was more like the top floor of the south side of the townhouse. It was expansive and decorated in rich, warm colors. Someone had lit the fireplace for them and filled a dresser and the closet with clothes for her. Her heart turned over in her chest seeing clothes for her, hanging next to what she assumed were his clothes. He had told her that DC was his home. He'd been vacationing in Lake George when she needed him, which she would always be thankful for. But really, they'd both been living in DC off and on for years. Her, mostly on. Him, when he wasn't on active duty. With the accident that claimed his brother and other teammates, he'd retired and was living fully in DC before he left for Lake George.

She walked from his bedroom into his bathroom, which had a wall of the same mullioned glass as the windows downstairs did. The view overlooked the gardens behind the house, and although they were fairly overgrown now, she imagined they could be stunning.

The bathroom was almost all marble and brass with soft, white towels hung for them. His shampoo and soap were in the giant walk-in shower. He sighed. "I'm actually super excited to be back here. I love this place and I can't wait to bend you over the bench in that shower." He followed her eyes back to the shower.

"Stop looking like that, Max, the guys have lunch laid out for us," she admonished.

"Baby, I'll never stop looking at you like this," he promised her.

She walked back over to him and circled her arms around him, leaning her head on his chest. "I love you, Max," she breathed into him.

"I love you too, Violet," he replied softly.

They did break apart then because they knew they had work to do and the guys did indeed have lunch laid out so they could get started. He grabbed her hand, looking down to see her little fingers eclipsed by his larger ones. "Tonight though, Vi, I intend to worship that sinful body of yours," he promised darkly.

They joined the others in a massive, bright eat-in kitchen around a Carrara marble island.

To Violet's surprise, Mila and Wills were also there. The computer screen had only given Vi a small glance at her new friends and she was taken aback at meeting both Mila and Wills. Mila was a petite, fair-skinned blonde with a cherub face. She had enormous blue eyes and seemed to be vibrating with her effusive energy. Wills was gorgeous, which seemed to be a prerequisite to be on Luke's team. His wide smile lit up his tan face, his deep-blue eyes lined with laugh lines. They looked like an ad for a beach vacation instead of the tech masters they were.

Mila almost choked her she hugged her so hard and Vi thought she was going to knock Max over with her affection and tears of apology. He assured her that it was all good countless times before Wills walked over and whispered in her ear. Her porcelain skin flamed scarlet and she murmured back to him, blue eyes shining. She then turned back to Violet and Max, smiling sheepishly.

"I'm just so thankful you're both OK," she said.

After the rest of the introductions were made, everyone started talking at once. It seemed like Max's entire team was there: Seb, Luke, Brian, Wills, Nate and Theo. They were only missing Tad, but he was due in later that day.

"This place looks like a *GQ* calendar shoot for Marine Heartthrobs," Hazel said to Mila and Violet. Mila giggled. "Try working with all of this hotness all of the time. It actually starts to hurt my eyes." All of the girls laughed.

"What's so funny down there, ladies?" Seb asked from the other end of the island.

"I was just in awe of the sexiness smothering the air here. I think I could get pregnant from just smelling all of this testosterone," Hazel said.

"Hazel, I'd be happy to show you a good time once we put this mess behind us," Theo said.

"Off limits!" Luke erupted, slamming his hand on the island. Everyone turned to stare at him, shocked faces from the ladies, all of the guys smirking. "You will not touch my sisters," he added.

"Shut it, Warden Luke-a-licious, I'm looking to lose my V card this year and maybe Theo can help me," she retorted, sticking her tongue out at him.

"Hazel!" Violet shouted at the same time awkward laughter erupted around the table. Everyone was laughing nervously at Hazel's comment. Well, everyone but Luke who looked murderous. He stood up and dropped his napkin onto his plate.

"Thanks for lunch, assholes, I'll be in command center." He stalked off while the laughter died down.

"Yes, thank you all so much for everything. I really don't know what to say. You've all done so much for me and for Hazel because of the mess I accidentally made," Vi said to all of them.

"Violet, it's all good. You didn't cause this, remember that. This isn't on you. Two things are also very clear to us. One, you belong to Max, so you are part of us. We have your back. Always. Two, these are some very bad guys, and we are doing our jobs to take care of them. And we will take care of them," Nate said. He'd been quiet so far, almost broody. But when he spoke, he said a great deal. He had the appearance of a silent mountain man, gruff and bearded on the exterior but warm and gooey inside.

Her eyes felt hot again, but she refused to cry in front of everyone again. "Well, you're all part of me now too, and Max belongs to me. So, let's go get this figured out so we can move on." She stood up. "Where is command center?"

They all cleaned up the lunch mess and went downstairs, the guys leading the way. Once down there, Max placed his palm on a reader by a nondescript door. A screen popped up and it scanned his face. Once that was complete, he typed in a password and the door clicked open. They all filed inside a dark, enormous space. It must have taken up more than the full basement of one townhouse. The walls were reinforced and there were screens lit on every corner of all four walls. It was like being in a 360 tower from every level of the house. Under those screens were desks along three walls of the room, taking the length of the wall and all showing surveillance feed of different areas.

"Oh!" Violet exclaimed. She'd found the screens on her parents. "Oh my God," she laughed. "We are being so invasive of their privacy!"

"There isn't a camera in their bedroom and bathroom, though they don't seem to keep activities to those areas if you know what I mean," Brian said.

"Ewwww," three voices replied at the same time. Luke, Vi, and Hazel looked at each other then, all grossed out.

"Don't worry, I know how to keep them safe and switch off certain feeds at certain times." Wills said.

"Well, thank God for small favors," Violet muttered.

They had screens showing the outside of Neil's property, currently surrounded by cleaning crew trucks, and wait a minute—

"Is that the inside of Ambassador Neil's townhome?" Vi asked.

Luke had been sitting along the desk with the feeds Violet was asking about and turned to smile smugly at her. "You do know that we are special forces, right? Raiders."

She had known that, but she hadn't really stopped to think about what that specifically meant before.

"Theo was over there earlier carrying in chairs and tables. Gotta use his muscles for something worthwhile. So, what if he got a little lost and dropped a few cameras?" Luke said. He was still glaring at Theo, but his voice was even.

"Wills is really the brains behind the tech. The cameras

and audio feeds are in essentially clear patches that can be affixed anywhere. They are the size of a nickel and, most importantly, can't be detected by any government, foreign or domestic. He's been building the prototypes since the boys 'retired,' and this is actually their first test run," Mila bragged about her friend to them.

"Wow, that is amazing, Wills, seriously incredible," Violet exclaimed.

"Buddy, this is amazing. Congrats, man, we knew you could do it." Max slapped Wills's back proudly as the other guys echoed their congratulations. She loved how they showed up for each other. They were family, and they were her family now too.

CHAPTER TWENTY NINE

MAX

Mila had been able to hack the guest list and add many of them to the guest list of the party. She'd added herself and Theo, posing as a young couple down from NYC. New money. Theo was probably the flashiest with his money, so that worked out well. Vi and Hazel would have been too recognizable and there was no way in hell he was letting Violet that close to Neil ever again. They'd argued about that. She had understood his position but she was struggling with Mila jumping into any danger on her behalf. Mila was the only woman they had who had never been photographed though, so she was their safest bet right now. Mila had assured Violet that she was excited to do it, she rarely "got to work in the field."

Tad and Luke would be on site also, going as themselves. Tad's family was part of the old DC crowd and Luke had made a name for himself with that investing prowess. No one really knew exactly how successful, but everyone could see he was some degree of good at it. They would be there as themselves mostly, but the playboy versions. Retired Marines who had found wealth and had nothing tying them anywhere. Mila had even found them dates through one of her CIA contacts. Both dates were regular informants and knew how to defend themselves if they needed to. Mila had taken care of that piece beautifully and the ladies were happy to jump in to help.

Wills would run cybersecurity from here at the house; Brian would be their driver; Violet, Max, and Hazel would watch from the screens for anything familiar, recording everything. Nate was on overwatch too as an insurance policy and Seb would be at the house with them as added security. Max wanted to bristle at that and send Seb with the others, but with a recent GSW, he wasn't full strength and Vi's safety was more important than his pride.

They'd just finished running through the positions when Tad joined them, looking like a full mob boss hottie in a three-piece suit. He had jet-black hair, tan skin, and almost-clear green eyes, and the guys liked to tease him about his modeling career if the Marines got too tough for him. He came right to Max and hugged him. Tad was always the most affectionate of the group.

"Man, I am so thankful Lauren saved your ugly ass. I am so grateful for this lady right here." He turned to Vi and scooped her up in his arms. "I am so grateful to you for saving my guy. I can see a lightness in him, I can hear it in his voice, and Lauren tells me he would have literally bled out if not for your bra and cold compresses." Tad hugged Vi hard to his chest. She laughed and hugged him back.

OK now, Max thought. A quick hug, that's Tad's love language. And yet, he kept hugging her.

"That's enough, Tad." Max said, standing up and pulling Violet away from his friend. "Let Vi breathe."

"OK, man, sorry. I can see you're a wee territorial, no problem." He kissed Vi on the cheek as she stepped back into Max's embrace.

Tad introduced himself to Hazel and sat down next to her, looking at Luke expectantly. "Tell us your plan, oh brainiac."

The plan was fairly straightforward. It was mostly a recon mission to see if all the players would be in the same space again and if they'd incriminate themselves on recorded audio, thinking they were safe in Ambassador Neil's house. Luke would also poke around the study during the party and Tad would keep an eye out for him. Everyone had agreed that they needed more puzzle pieces to set an effective trap.

Luke had asked a few of their other buddies who they'd run special ops with, team guys from the SEALs, to monitor the New York and New Jersey port. Brody, who was covering Mr. and Mrs. Burke, was part of that team and those guys had really done them all a solid with their surveillance and willingness to help. Like Max and his guys, they had all agreed on one thing, these assholes needed stopped and this was what they'd signed up for.

Callum, the Seal team lead, had checked in late that afternoon with Luke, and Luke had pulled him up on the screen. "All good here, no unknown shipments, and we've verified each and every one of them," Callum reported.

"We've got tech on every nook and cranny. I promise you we will know if they try to move anything," Callum promised them solemnly.

They reviewed positions a few more times and talked about contingencies.

"Is bringing in Callum too much? I feel like we could have them there for nothing," Violet asked Max quietly.

"That's the military training though, sweetheart. You plan to fail. We use an acronym, PACE. You need a primary plan, an alternate plan, a contingency plan, and an emergency plan for your communications and for things like this. Having eyes there while we cover the players here is a necessary part of the cascading plan," he reassured her.

"These guys have proven they also have training, skills, funds, and access. There really is no limit to what we need to plan for," he went on. He could see that she was worried, she kept chewing on her bottom lip.

"It'll be OK, we've got you. Now stop chewing on something I intend to suck later," he said to her.

CHAPTER THIRTY

VIOLET

They ran through the positions, distress signals, and some hand signals a dozen more times and then all went upstairs to eat a late dinner together. She felt exhausted and couldn't believe this was her real life.

Dinner was actually a really light affair. They were easy in each other's company, telling stories about their tours together and their leaves. They talked about the fun times, the wild times, and the sad times. They all drank a toast to those brothers they'd lost. She saw Max run his hand across his pec muscle and knew he was missing Alex.

After dinner, everyone went their separate ways. Violet had wanted to talk more to Hazel, but Hazel had waved her off from the couch in front of the main fireplace. "Vi, please let me just read for now. I know we're going to talk about it but not here. Not yet. I'm too raw on this right now, and frankly, one of us should be upstairs getting her brains fucked out by her tall, dark, and handsome man."

"Hazey, for blurting out the virgin bit, you sure are comfortable talking about me getting some," she chided her.

"Yeah well, I have to live vicariously through you. I've been reading the same smutty romance novels you have, sis. One of us is now living it, so please, do us both a favor and go live it," Hazel grumped at her.

Violet kissed her sister on the forehead and went up to Max's apartment within the large house. Max had been helping clean up the kitchen when she came up, so she decided to start the shower. She lowered the lights in the room to a beautiful rose-gold glow and walked into the glass enclosure.

No sooner had she stepped fully under the hot spray, she heard him come into the room.

"Starting without me, Vi?" he asked her darkly as he shed his clothes.

She felt a deep clench between her legs at his roughly growled words. She felt his question against her skin and she turned to face him, lathering her hands in silky soap. He looked practically feral staring at her, and she wondered briefly how far she could push him with teasing. She brought her hands to her breasts and began to knead them under his watchful eye. She started gently, gliding her ring finger along the undersides of her breasts before cupping them and squeezing them together.

He'd taken his cock in his hand as he watched her, stroking from root to tip lazily.

She rolled her nipples with both of her hands and then slowly worked one of her hands down her thighs. She soaped herself, his eyes tracing every move before she stepped back under the spray and rinsed the bubbles off.

He stepped into the glass enclosure and kissed her roughly before spinning her around and stepping tightly behind her. She must have hit the limit of the teasing he'd take. His hands grabbed hers and moved them back to her breasts, using her own hands under his to mold and tickle and pinch. He kept at that until she began to squirm and then he reached above her and pulled the shower wand from its magnetic base. He flipped on the other shower heads to keep water on them and keep her warm as he lowered the shower wand down the front of her.

"Let's get you very clean, Vi, so I can get you very fucking dirty," he rasped in her ear. He popped the lobe of her ear into his hot mouth and suckled.

She shuddered against him, her wetness coating her legs. "Keep up that torture on those gorgeous tits of yours, baby."

He pressed the wand against her pussy and she came violently against his hand as soon as he added a finger to her clit. Her ass was tucked against him so tightly, he felt her orgasm crash through her entire being, but he still didn't stop.

He aimed the warm water deep inside of her and worked her with his fingers, simultaneously biting the back of her neck just enough to make her shiver uncontrollably.

"Please, please, please," she begged as her legs shook against him. He returned the wand to its magnetic base, then swept his hands down her body, grabbing her hands. He pulled them up and placed them on the marble wall above her head and then swept his hands back down to her hips.

"Don't move those hands, baby," he said.

He notched against her and filled her completely. She cried out and dropped her head back onto his shoulder. His left hand played with her clit lazily while he ground into her, hard. His right hand rolled along her nipples, and he whispered dark and erotic promises into her ears, nibbling along her neck.

"I'm coming again. Max!" Her body bowed against his, her juices flowing over his hand and down her legs. He bit down on the sensitive skin where her neck met her shoulder and erupted inside of her. His hips were moving of their own accord as he braced his palms against the backs of her hands above their heads. He shivered as he finished emptying into her.

He lowered their arms together and spun her around to face him. He kissed her deeply, his firm, full lips nibbling and sucking at hers.

Her body spasmed again, aftershocks crashing through her.

"Max. That was . . ." she started.

"Everything, Vi. That was everything." He hugged her to him.

He dried her off lovingly and pulled her to bed. They snuggled under the covers, and she pushed back into him. She'd never known life could be like this. She hadn't known what she hadn't known. He had given her this hold into heaven, and she was going to protect him and this love at all costs.

CHAPTER THIRTY ONE

VIOLET

The morning of the event dawned overcast and a bit gloomy. The mood among them was focused. She had to remember that for all of the love and laughter displayed among these men, they were still warriors. Battle-hardened warriors.

Violet and Max spent most of the day watching the video feeds off and on with Hazel. The Neil house was a beehive of activity preparing for the party and there were lots of players to keep track of. They had everything recording also so that they could review the videos in the coming days, pouring over the details of the puzzle.

Violet and Hazel helped Mila get ready for the party and Vi gave her an overview of the party in Saratoga Springs. If it ran the same way, they would take phones and check for any signals. So far, the tech Wills had designed had held on undetected. They had great visuals and decent audio. Obviously, each member of their team would also be outfitted with as many of the little clear patches as possible.

Luke was running through plans, both primary and alternate, with everyone one last time in the foyer when Callum checked in on Luke's phone.

"Lots of activity here this afternoon. We're checking everything we can, but the volume has almost quadrupled. Some of the containers we've checked are just crates upon crates of empty boxes with ticking clocks and baking supplies mixed in throughout," Callum delivered the bad news.

"Shit. They're preparing to move whatever product they've got. This is a classic and pretty smart giant fucking shell game," Max said.

"I think it means we have the right port. They don't know where Vi is and if she knows what she has on them. She hasn't turned on her phone, so they have good reason to believe she hasn't seen the video snap she took. They know someone has helped her get away multiple times and is pretty good at keeping her hidden," Luke said.

"At this scale, they probably can't shift the timing of their product, so they have to do whatever they can to deter anyone helping her," Seb added. "The empty containers at that volume is pretty evil genius."

"It is, particularly with the clocks, sugar, and flour. It's a real mind fuck for the humans and dogs on my team," Callum added.

"So, what do we do?" Violet asked.

"We stay the course for now," Max reassured her. "The team here will continue with the recon mission, the team there will continue checking shipping containers, and we reconnect when one of us knows more."

He enfolded her in his arms, his chin resting on her head. "Soon, sweetheart. This will all be over soon."

She felt sick watching everyone prepare for the party. She understood that this was reconnaissance and that they'd done this literally hundreds of times, she just had a knot in her gut. These people had quickly come to mean everything to her, they were Max's family, and he couldn't take losing more of his family.

She looked over at Luke, getting ready to head out. "Please be safe, Luke, I need you all to be safe," she pleaded.

He nodded at her. "I know, Vi, we've got this." There were hugs and some sniffles from Vi and Hazel before Tad and Luke left in one car, windows blacked out, Mila and Theo in another car, also armored and windows blacked out. Both cars looked like normal sedans from the outside, middle-of-the-road level sedans at that. Nate had left that morning to prepare and have his primary and alternate positions. He was in his hide site now. They were short manpower tonight, though, without Max doing either overwatch with him or spotting.

All of them would actually switch cars three more times before pulling up in front of the event. Luke and Tad would hit the W bar before they went over to give the appearance they wanted to portray, and Mila and Theo had reservations at Le Diplomate for a "quick drink" before they went over. There were hotel rooms saved in five different hotels for each set. They could play the shell game too. They wanted to ensure the safety of their team and also that of their home base.

Violet found herself, Hazel, Max, and Seb tied to the screens in command center, all of them anxious to see if tonight would bring them the breakthrough they needed.

Max checked in with the team in the field, "Clocked Philip arriving. No Brady, but Philip has a date with him."

A chorus of "copy" sounded throughout their comms feeds.

Mila and Theo arrived first as they had planned. They played their parts perfectly, arriving in style in a new Jag F-Type coup in a custom shade of graphite. Theo stepped out at the valet in front of Ambassador Neil's historic townhome, quickly rounding the Jag to open Mila's door and take her hand, helping her out. They looked perfect and so glamorous, Vi almost felt like she was watching a reality TV show showcasing the young, rich, and fabulous.

Everyone in command central held their breath until the couple was through security safely. Their comms were working so far, which was good news. They began to mingle, drinks in hand.

Theo pulled Mila close. To the average observer, it probably looked like he was nuzzling her neck. Which, actually, he was, but he was also speaking into the little tech patch behind her ear, which her hair covered.

"All the players are here. Visual on Philip and Ambassador Neil."

"Copy," Max said. "The feeds are holding, we see them also."

The party filled up quickly after that, both Mila and Theo doing their best to nonchalantly stick close to Philip or Neil without being around too much.

"Theo, cool it. Your acting is a little much, man," Wills grumbled over the comms to Theo. The cameras they had access to showed Theo smirking down at Mila even more after that as he snuggled in closer to her, kissing her ear.

CHAPTER THIRTY TWO

MAX

By the time Luke and Tad arrived with their dates, the party was in full swing. They'd had an Uber Black drop them off and both appeared to be very intoxicated. Max knew the drill, they'd both reek of booze too. A very old trick from a very old book, but it worked. Their dates were dressed to kill and also appeared to be very tipsy.

They hadn't gotten anything good yet. Hell, they hadn't even seen Philip and Neil together and they had eyes practically everywhere. The party was at its busiest and still nothing, thus it was time to start the next phase of their plan.

"It's time," Max said into the comms feeds.

"Copy," Luke whispered as he took another drink. He excused himself from his group of Tad and their dates, making sure to look congenial and drunk.

Luke pretended to stumble down one of the hallways of the mansion, away from most of the guests. They heard Luke over the comms mumbling as he passed other guests, "You know where the head is around here?" No one really engaged with him, but it fit the pattern you'd expect from a rich party boy.

Comms showed Philip still in the thick of the party, but Ambassador Neil was no longer visible. Max had a bad feeling in his gut about all of this. They had two account recipients that they didn't know tied to the ambassador. Even if one was definitively Philip, they didn't really know who the other player was. There was something they were missing. He just hoped that they got the intel tonight to figure it out.

Luke had been their team leader forever. He knew what to do if he "stumbled" upon pay dirt here. Hell, they needed the pay dirt.

A beautiful woman came into view in the hallway Luke had just entered. They could only see so much with the patch on Luke and the patches placed in that hallway but they could see the woman was upset. She had cried out loudly and paused against the hallway, covering her face, her body racked with loud, gasping sobs.

"She looks so familiar," Vi murmured from his side.

"Sir, sir, please. I need help." The woman shuddered again.

It felt off to Max, something was wrong. "Tad, I think we have a situation for Luke in the hallway," he said into the comms.

"Copy," Tad replied tersely.

Luke had gone to the woman's side. "Miss, it's OK." His arms went to her shoulders loosely and attempted to help her stand up. "It's OK," he said again.

"That's Ilyana!" Violet yelled in command center. "That's Philip's date from Saratoga Springs."

It was too late. Ilyana straightened, plunging the knife hidden in her hand in Luke's gut. He staggered to the wall and tried to catch himself. His hands went to the knife, blood running over his hands.

"Hazelnut," Luke whispered as he hit the wall, unconscious.

CHAPTER THIRTY THREE

MAX

Max heard Vi and Hazel screaming at the screens. Tad came into the hallway as Ilyana stepped around Luke. He tried to rush to Luke, but Ilyana stopped him. Her smile was cold and her eyes were hard on his face.

"Perfect timing to help your friend," she smiled. The patch on the wall showed a man behind Tad, and the gun held to the back of his head.

"Easy now, killer, we'll be taking a little walk." She turned and the mercenary behind Tad jammed the gun harder into the back of his head. "Follow me, please," she directed. Tad began to walk after her as another man came into the hallway and began dragging Luke after them.

"Mila, get out!" Wills had yelled into the room, knowing the comms would pick up the warning. "Theo, get your asses out, it's a trap," Wills shouted again.

Neither replied, their patches showing them both heading toward the door, Theo's arm protectively around Mila as they made polite excuses to leave. Mila shook his arm off and reached for the dates she had arranged for Tad and Luke, motioning them to the door.

The four of them cleared the doorway and made it to be bottom of the steps, signaling to Nate they were clear. Brian was rounding the corner as fast as possible to pick them up. Shouts sounded from the top of the stairs behind them.

"Clear for shot," Nate rumbled lowly. The man at the top

of the stairs in pursuit of Mila and Theo went down as he said it. Nate picked off two more as Brian slowed the SUV and shoved open the door from inside. Both Luke's and Tad's dates for the evening jumped in first.

Theo had practically picked Mila up by then and they jumped toward the open door. Having never fully stopped, the car took off down the street with Theo pulling the door closed as they went. Per their protocol, they'd go to an alternate location and connect in via tech. It was too hot to get back right then and they were in triage. Nate would be moving to the next location if it was safe to do so.

Seb was in motion in command central, strapping a bulletproof vest on and adding knives to his leg straps when they heard dark laughter. The patches on Tad and Luke showed that they'd been dragged and ushered into the library of the mansion where Philip, Ilyana, and Ambassador Neil stood.

Max counted four hired guns with them and all of them looked knowledgeable about the guns they had fixed on his brothers. They'd tied Tad's hands behind his back.

Luke grunted at Tad's feet, slowly coming to, and Tad kneeled carefully to check on him. "He needs medical care, please," Tad pleaded with their captors.

"This isn't fucking amateur hour, Luke, we know you're connected to Violet Burke. You may think you buried that connection but you can't bury physical photographs in frames along random mantels, now can you?" Neil pulled Luke's head back viciously by the hair.

"Really, that was our break. Thank God that dumb bitch sister had that one photo of the three of you in her apartment. I was getting nervous, and then like a giant fucking Christmas gift, there was a link. You may have hidden the person, but her photo gave you up." Ambassador Neil laughed.

"And now, here you are at my party. The gifts keep coming. You thought you could waltz in my house and ruin my deal? Wrong fucking plan!" he bellowed against Luke's face, spittle landing on his cheek.

Max could see the blood seeping against Luke's fingers and knew they would be out of time soon to save him.

"So now, we're going to wait for our little friend to arrive. She'll come out if you tell her to, and that's what you're going to do."

"Over my dead body, asswipe," Luke raged raggedly, his lips tight in pain.

Ambassador Neil laughed maniacally, "Oh, for sure your dead body is going to be part of this, but so is hers. Better get her here soon, looks like the hourglass is going to run out on you. I could also shoot Tad here to speed this up but I really don't want to have to do that here."

Ambassador Neil held the muzzle of a gun hard against Tad's forehead now.

"Bring me the goddamn phone!"

His guttural voice had scraped across her skin through the comms.

"Load me up, Max, I'm going with you," Violet's firm voice interrupted his preparations.

He stared at her while Seb started to hand her a vest to put under her sweatshirt.

"No. We are not exposing you in that way. Babe, you're a writer, not a Marine, not trained for the CIA, no BUDs background, please, Violet. I can't lose you and Luke would rather die than have you at risk, as would Tad," he pleaded with her.

"Max, I have to do this. I couldn't live with myself if Luke died for me or if something happens to Tad. That's not who I am. You're a warrior and I love that about you. But, Max, I am too, and I am going with you."

"She needs to do this, Max, we can cover her, you know we can." Seb looked at him. "And we need to do this now if we're going to carry it off."

Max yanked Violet to him and crushed his lips to hers. "You will not die, Violet. I intend to marry you and fill your arms with dark-haired babies. You will be OK," he commanded.

"I won't die, Max, you won't let me, just like I won't let you. Let's go get our family," she promised him.

Hazel had been stunned from the moment Luke had been stabbed. She hugged her sister to her fiercely and whispered a hurried, "I love you, please bring him back to me. Please come back to me."

Sebastian left ahead of Violet and Max. Nate had checked in from his alternate shot location and was ready for them.

The party had raged on, most of DC's elite completely unaware of the situation in the library and on the front steps earlier. The music was loud, it was late, and the alcohol had been flowing freely. They had no idea that they were in tall grass with dangerous snakes. Hell, most parties in DC probably had a completely alternate thing happening.

A guard at the door ushered Max and Violet in as soon as they cleared the top of the steps. He immediately whisked them through a locked door off the foyer into a formal parlor. He locked the door behind them and checked them for weapons. The man took the gun at Max's back under his coat and patted his legs for knives. He'd started to pat Vi's legs down too, with Max growling at him.

"Let's go, asshole," Max said.

The guy just laughed at him and opened French doors along the wall, leading to the library they'd seen on comms.

"Luke!" Violet ran to him, placing her hands on his wound. She sat on her haunches and cradled his head.

"What the fuck, Max?" he gasped, barely conscious.

"It's OK, buddy, she wanted to help." Max winked at Luke. He knew Tad would be ready once he saw the wink.

The thing about their training is that they'd had an alternate plan, a contingency place and, of course, an emergency plan. They knew something was bound to go FUBAR, it always did to some degree.

"Give me the phone, Ms. Burke." Ambassador Neil held out his hand to her.

"Why are you doing this?" she cried. Max had never seen her look so fragile. His Violet, she was so fucking smart. If he didn't know her better, he would believe her act of falling apart too.

"Why?" she cried again. Tad looked over at him.

"You just had to take that fucking snap, Vi. We had a great thing rolling, a really profitable thing, actually. I don't mind telling you because it is pretty genius, if I do say so myself. And, in case you were wondering, none of you are leaving here alive anyway, except maybe Tad. I mean, he'll have a drunken accident later tonight, but it won't be here. Daddy would be too suspicious and I don't want him on my ass," Ambassador Neil said.

"Weapons from Pell Weaponry go out of the port of New York, like always, just a few containers less. Those containers go on a different ship, owned by the lovely Ilyana's little shipping company. Those go into Tunisia and, from there, to my buyers. We all make money. Lots of money. Too much money for you to fuck up our operation," Neil continued to brag.

"But what could I possibly have captured on my snap?" Violet asked, fear making her voice raspy.

"Ilyana, Brandon, Philip, Brady, and me all in one place. That, my dear, only happens once a year and you happened to capture it. There is no reason for all of us to be connected, outside of our little operation. You did me a favor though." He shrugged his shoulders. "Brandon had started to get greedy, and your little episode gave me a great excuse to take care of that." His eyes had taken on a flat, unfocused look. He was mad.

"Where's your brother?" Max asked Philip, turning to him. He angled his body toward Philip, causing him to shift just enough to the left, right in front of the window.

Philip laughed and shrugged. "Fuck if I know, he's not needed for this."

A shot rang out, shattering the glass behind Philip. As

Ilyana turned toward the window, Philip fell to the floor, a bullet wound straight through the back of his head. He was dead before he hit the ground, and Ilyana ran to him, screaming.

Luke took that moment to use the last of his waning strength to throw the knife he'd shimmied out of the back of Violet's bra strap when she'd cradled his head. It flew true, straight into Ambassador Neil's neck. He, too, dropped to the floor, the life gurgling from him, his hands clutching the knife.

Theo had followed Nate's shot in and threw a gun to Max as he took out three of the guards in the room. Max shot the other as Tad grabbed Luke and began carrying him from the room. Rookie fucking mistake to tie his hands behind his back where he could get free of them without anyone seeing him do so.

Ilyana let out a guttural scream and lunged for Violet. She grabbed her by the hair and backed toward the fireplace, bringing up her arm with a knife in her hand. She held it to Violet's neck.

"Weapons down, or I swear to God, I will gut her in front of you," she raged. She sliced Vi right above her collarbone. Violet's wide eyes found his. He could tell she was trying to tamp down her fear. She kept her eyes locked on him.

Tad had dragged Luke out to the waiting Seb. He knew Nate was still in position, but Ilyana wouldn't budge from in front of the fireplace. There was no way he had a clear shot.

"Drop it!" Ilyana screamed, pressing the tip of the knife deeper into Violet's neck. There was a deep red drip starting where she had started cutting, a steady rivulet into Violet's sweatshirt. The neckline had a growing crimson bloom.

Max nodded to Theo and they both dropped their guns. "OK! Stop cutting there." He raised his hands back up. "Please stop cutting."

Ilyana screamed at him, "He's dead. He was my life and you killed him!" She dragged the knife further across Vi's neck, almost to her jugular.

"Max." Violet whispered his name.

"Sweetheart," he said, his eyes pleading with her to stay strong.

"I love you, Max, in every lifetime we have," she vowed. Her eyes were steady on his, a look of determination taking over.

She reached down, grabbed the fire poker next to her leg, and swung it up as hard as she could. The force knocked both her and Ilyana back toward the roaring fire.

Max lunged for Violet, catching her sweatshirt just before Ilyana pulled her into the fire with her. Her neck was gushing blood, having been cut a little more when she jerked the poker up.

Ilyana screamed from the fireplace, engulfed in flames. Max crushed Violet to his chest, sweeping her into his arms and turning toward the door. She needed care immediately, she was losing so much blood. He nodded at Theo as Theo picked his gun off from the floor and shot Ilyana.

CHAPTER THIRTY FOUR

VIOLET

She could hear sirens screaming everywhere around them. Max had yet to put her down, carrying her through the hallway and out the front door. FBI agents were swarming everywhere, and she heard Max screaming for an ambulance.

He'd ripped off his shirt and had it held to her neck as he carried her. "Hold this tightly, baby, you will not die," he demanded of her.

She tried to reassure him but found that her voice didn't work well. She felt so tired. She tried to keep her eyes open, she needed to see Luke. She needed to reassure Max that she was going to be fine.

"Love you, Max," she whispered against his chest, her arms going limp.

"Violet!" She heard Max yelling at her, but it was from so far away. She wanted to rest where she was and wait for him to get to her. Darkness overtook her.

It was dark and quiet when she regained consciousness. She could hear beeping all around her and her throat felt as if she'd swallowed gravel. She lifted her hands and ran her fingertips along the bandages around her neck and across her collarbone. Her hands had wires coming out, IVs and other monitors attached. Well, that explained all of the beeping.

There was a low light from a lamp to her left and a warm, solid weight against her legs. She glanced to her side and saw Max's dark head laid on the bed next to where her hand had been, sleeping on his folded forearms. She laid her hand on his head. "Max," she whispered.

He jolted awake, his sleepy eyes taking her in. "Vi, sweetheart, am I dreaming?"

She rasped out a laugh, groaning slightly at the pain that caused in her throat.

"Baby, careful, you've had a rough night. You scared us all. The doctor said to take it easy on the talking for the next few days." He laid his hand across her chest. "Luke's going to be OK, babe. He went through a great deal of blood and he has a lot of R&R coming, but he's a tough son of a bitch. Hazel has been bouncing back and forth between your rooms."

"Everyone?" She tried to ask.

"Everyone else is OK. Tad's pissed they got the jump on us, but he'll be OK. Speaker Mills and his family are being detained and questioned, but so far, it looks like they're in the dark about their son's activities. Callum and his team picked up Brady in the city, and right now, he's cooling his heels deep inside a CIA stronghold. We got them all."

"The guns?" she mouthed, scared of his answer.

"Callum and his guys found four shipping containers being loaded on one of Ilyana's ships. The weapons have been confiscated and a thorough investigation is underway," he assured her.

She motioned for him to help her, so he raised her bed slightly. "You need a drink, babe? I've got you." He brought a straw to her lips. The cool water trickling down her abused throat felt like heaven.

It was then that she saw what the warm weight against her legs was. Blitz! The dog was quietly watching them, love shining in his eyes.

Violet felt tears leaking out of her own eyes. "I love you boys."

"Good, Vi, because we need you. Marry me. Be ours." Max

quietly spoke to her, his hands gathering hers. "Please, sweetheart, be my wife."

"In every lifetime, yes," she promised him, her voice cracking.

EPILOGUE

MAX

Blitz was wagging his tail and barking happily at the door to the underground garage when Max walked by. Tad must finally be here. That guy was always MIA lately and so secretive. He was going to be on his ass about that, he knew something was brewing for his brother.

The rest of the group had gathered in the library around the fireplace with food and drinks. He and Vi had been living there full time as had Luke and Hazel, in separate areas, and they'd put up a Christmas tree in that room for everyone to gather around. His girl loved Christmas and having everyone together.

They'd flown down to Pensacola Beach, once Vi felt up to it, and told her parents about what had happened. They'd been aghast and terrified for their daughters and Luke. It had taken a long time for them to stop hugging Violet and Hazel and they'd been desperate to see Luke, who had stayed behind recuperating in DC.

Lawrence and Nancy Burke had arrived two days ago and were settled in the Dupont Circle mansion with them for the holidays. Luke had been recovering well and was anxious to be full strength. His workouts were getting longer and longer and Max knew his friend would be back in action soon.

Hazel was moving out after the new year, ready to be back on her own. She and Vi had been having a great time planning the wedding, even though the ordeal had changed Hazel.

She was quieter now and whatever was going on with her and Luke seemed to have slowed down. He made a mental note to ask Vi about that as there were no secrets between them.

Blitz was so happy to have everyone gathering, the little shit kept sneaking food from everyone.

He waited for Tad to walk in so they could go in the library together.

"Brother, you're always late or MIA lately, tell me what's up," Max said as soon as the door opened.

"Hey, Max! Let a guy get in the door before the inquisition starts. Aren't you buried in Violet all the time lately? How do you know my schedule?" Tad deferred.

Max slapped him on the back as they walked into the library. "Being buried in Violet makes me smarter, not dumber. Don't think I'm dropping this."

"Yeah, it's time. I want to bring the team together and talk soon," Tad replied.

"No time like the present, Tad," Max said.

"Max, I know that Vi will murder us all if we keep the gift exchange waiting any longer. Hurry up. Geez, slacker." He kept walking into the room, making his way to Vi so he could sweep her up in a hug.

That fucker. Max rolled his eyes and made his way to the chair next to the fireplace where Vi was standing.

"OK, guys, let's get this party started!" she exclaimed, a cushion cut diamond ring sparkling brightly on her ring fin-ger as she clapped her hands together. He'd chosen a cushion cut because legend had it that the ring was designed to sparkle in candlelight. His girl loved romance and history, so it was perfect. He couldn't believe the ugliness she'd been through had led her to him. It was their silver lining. She'd saved him from the darkness of loss, and he'd saved her from monsters out to silence her.

"Max first!" Luke shouted.

"Max already got Vi this year, no fair!" Seb hollered, laughing.

"I did indeed. I am the luckiest bastard here," Max smugly replied.

"Babe, you get to go first. Luke called it and he's the team lead," Violet reasoned as she handed him a beautifully wrapped gift the size of a shirt box.

"What my lady wants, my lady gets." He kissed her hand.

The group quieted down a little while he unwrapped, watching to see what he had received. The box was really light, and when he shook it, it didn't make a sound.

He popped open the box and found a little black-and-white photo inside. It looked like a fuzzy black-and-white picture of a bean. He looked up questioningly, everyone's eyes glued to him.

"Max, babe. I know you said you wanted to start trying . . ." Violet started.

"Leave that part out, Vi." Luke groaned.

"Vi? Sweetheart? Is this what I think it is?" Max asked, his hand shaking on the picture.

"Yes, we're going to have a baby, Max."

He scooped her up before she finished responding and whooped out a yell of joy. "We're having a baby!" He set her down and kissed her deeply.

"I thought maybe we could name the baby Alex," she said, happy tears sliding down her face.

"Oh, Violet, thank you. Thank you for being everything to me. I love you."

"In every lifetime, Max." She kissed him again as their friends and family cheered for them, Blitz barking happily along with them all.

ACKNOWLEDGMENTS

I want to thank my family first. My husband and our boys have been great sports through this process and are excited for me to chase this lifelong dream of being a writer. Thank you boys for being the strong foundation for me to do this. Thank you also to my parents, brother, aunts and uncles, and in-laws for the years of patience while I had my head buried in a book. Love you all.

A huge thank you to my cousins. Kim and Melissa did some last-minute editing that was clutch! I incorporated almost all of their edits. Lis, I'm sorry I wasn't technically correct on the Challenger 3500. Folks, you need two pilots for that, just to be clear. My guys are military badasses though, so I took some liberties. Kimmy also served as a technical advisor with input from her Marine husband, as well as a research assistant during an unforgettable trip to Kansas City. Love you both so much.

Canyon and Sydney helped with planning and naming my LLC, which I write under. Thank you both for the advice, I love you.

Courtney and Suni helped with a pen name and all kinds of other research. Suni also took headshots for me when I was scared out of my mind about this new venture. Love you ladies so much.

A huge thank you also to Christie and Harley, for supporting me to get this published. Your recommendations, connections, kindness, love and laughter were just what I needed. You, Ollie, and your team at Red Fern Booksellers are amazing. You are all creating something so beautiful in our community and I love you all. Cheers to more kitten rescues.

My humble thanks to all of my friends and family who

have offered tremendous support and encouragement. You have all played a part of me having the courage to do this and I am so grateful to be in this village. Thank you.

Thank you also to all of the actual badasses and their incredible families who serve our country.

ABOUT ATMOSPHERE PRESS

Founded in 2015, Atmosphere Press was built on the principles of Honesty, Transparency, Professionalism, Kindness, and Making Your Book Awesome. As an ethical and author-friendly hybrid press, we stay true to that founding mission today.

If you're a reader, enter our giveaway for a free book here:

SCAN TO ENTER
BOOK GIVEAWAY

If you're a writer, submit your manuscript for consideration here:

SCAN TO SUBMIT
MANUSCRIPT

And always feel free to visit Atmosphere Press and our authors online at atmospherepress.com. See you there soon!

ABOUT THE AUTHOR

Photo credit to the brilliant, lovely, and talented Suni Michaelsen

AMY COLE is a voracious romance reader residing with her husband, two teenage sons, two black Labs, and one grouchy cat in the Midwest. She is a lover of history, books of all types, food, cooking, traveling, her family, sports-specifically college football and anything the Kansas State Wildcats are competing in, decorating her house, and being outside (primarily in the fall and winter). She loves watching her boys and their friends play football and basketball and run track.

She considers her family and friends as the best part of life and works to weave easter eggs into her stories for each and every one of them.

Prior to starting her writing career, Amy traveled extensively for work for many years. She's tried to include fun tidbits about great locations and can always be counted on to offer advice on where to eat for anyone traveling to a new city.

This is a debut novel in a planned series. Amy promises spice, historical tidbits, those fun easter eggs, some mystery, lots of happily ever afters, and that no dogs (or cats) will be too badly harmed in any story she writes.